Praise for *Resurrection Girls*

★ "A refined, startling debut that brims with authorial skill… Every line is crafted in a tender way and with obvious skill. The text is full of slick metaphors and genuine introspection. Literary without being too verbose, the sheer language of the story qualifies it as a fantastic read." —*Foreword*, starred review

"The lovely, assured prose draws on ancient archetypes and a lingering sense of dread to pave the way for a strange but satisfying conclusion…a heartbreaking but hopeful exploration of death and grief." —*Kirkus Reviews*

"A raw, captivating exploration of grief, friendship, and the reclamation of life."—*Booklist*

"*Resurrection Girls* is a powerful examination of grief and loss, captivatingly woven with magic and ultimately hope. A compassionately rendered debut." —Emily A. Duncan, *New York Times* bestselling author of *Wicked Saints* and *Ruthless Gods*

"Ava Morgyn's passion and tenderness shine like a candle, guiding readers through the darkness of Olivia's story. Her compelling characters are made all the more real by the eerie undertow of myth. A beautiful, deeply emotional debut!" —Sarah Porter, author of *Vassa in the Night* and *Never-Contented Things*

"*Resurrection Girls* is a heartbreak of a book, where love and loss write letters to the strange things that lurk in the darkness. It's a stunning story that blends the inexplicable and the beautiful with the bittersweet." —Rin Chupeco, author of *Wicked As You Wish* and The Bone Witch trilogy

"A raw, poignant, unflinching examination of grief and healing wrapped up in a compelling story. *Resurrection Girls* is a brilliant debut." —C.J. Redwine, *New York Times* bestselling author of the Ravenspire series

RESURRECTION GIRLS

AVA MORGYN

ALBERT WHITMAN & COMPANY
CHICAGO, ILLINOIS

Library of Congress Cataloging-in-Publication
data is on file with the publisher.

Hardcover edition first published in the United States of America
in 2019 by Albert Whitman & Company
Paperback edition first published in the United States of America
in 2020 by Albert Whitman & Company
ISBN 978-0-8075-6940-5 (paperback)
ISBN 978-0-8075-6941-2 (ebook)

Printed in the United States of America
10 9 8 7 6 5 4 3 2 1 LSC 24 23 22 21 20

Cover art and book design by Aphelandra Messer

For more information about Albert Whitman & Company,
visit our website at www.albertwhitman.com.

For Evelyn.
We are one heart.

CHAPTER 1

The summer they moved in was the hottest on record since 1980. June, July, and August raged with hundred-degree days and the kind of steam-pot humidity Houston had come to be known for. Despite the wall of urban perspiration that greeted every citizen at every door, every morning across the city, we were knee deep in an unprecedented drought that had meteorologists twittering like canaries in coal mines. Looking back, maybe I should have known. Maybe the heat and the drought—the boil—were all signs, if you believe in such things. By then, however, by that desperate, cloying, relentless summer, my family had ceased to believe in anything.

It was three years to the day that the moving truck pulled into the cracked, weed-ridden driveway across the street. There was something wrong with June 9. Something that set that day apart from others. Something that caused it to stew in its own juices. A day of ferment. Three years before, on that same fated date, my three-year-old brother had drowned in our backyard pool. My parents had since had it filled in—a great, devastating show of jackhammers, wheelbarrows, and truck beds full of soil. The final act in a tragic play we were now trapped in. The closing curtain: a layer of fresh-laid sod. Our yard was now a giant grave to all the memories we would deny, all the words we refused to speak.

You could never trust a day divisible by that many threes.

And so, when their sixteen-foot moving truck pulled in across the street with *Haul It Your Way* plastered down the side in faded orange-and-blue letters, I should have known a mountain of shit was coming our way. I should have seen the cracks beginning to mark the dam and read our fate in their design. But it was hard to see past the curtain we'd closed over our lives, past the green lawn, where my little brother had once played and died, past the giant oak withering in our front yard—a testament to summer's brutality—past the smothering heat and the suffocating grief that surrounded us like the ash of Pompeii. It's a wonder I noticed them at all.

Of course, they were pretty hard to miss. From the beginning, there was something separate about them. They and June 9 deserved each other.

I was sixteen, with no car, which meant I was trapped inside the hollow, ringing, soulless structure we once called home. School was out, and without my studies to throw my energy and attention into, I was restless. I prowled. I stirred within the confines of our house with dust motes for company. My mother was upstairs in her room, locked behind her blackout curtains, wandering the land of the dead in a haze of OxyContin and Xanax. That's what she paid the ferryman with—prescription drugs. At best, they made her absent. At worst, they made her mean. My dad was…well, he was out. In truth, I didn't know where he was when he wasn't at work and wasn't at home. Neither my mom nor I did. He was just gone mostly. And when he was home, he wasn't present, so it didn't matter.

That house across the street had been vacant for years. It was a foreclosure. A Victorian wannabe with wood siding and a wraparound porch that made it seem older than the other houses on our street. The last family who'd lived there, a widowed mom with four kids, whose husband hung himself in the master bedroom, left it completely trashed inside. Once when I was a kid, long before Robby died, my mother used her real estate license to get the code on the lockbox. Curious and nosy, we let ourselves in and looked around.

"Shame," she'd said, running her squared nails over holes in the Sheetrock and gouges in the countertops. Mom was polished then. Professional. I watched her key in the code and used it to sneak back in. I would dare myself to go up to the master bedroom, get as high as the top step on the staircase, then the moment I'd hear a noise of some kind—a squeak or a groan—go running back out again.

We thought the tragedy and the bank's high asking price had rendered it untouchable. That was before we understood the ease with which tragedy could strike, before our own personal family tragedy blossomed like a corpse flower in our midst. Now, the two homes squared off across from each other, both vacant for all intents and purposes. Both haunted by their own ghosts.

Until they moved in.

Three women. Correction—three *generations* of women. A single mom, her daughter, who looked roughly my age, and the rheumatic grandmother, blind in both eyes and frail as bat bones. I watched them unload the moving truck from between the blackout curtains in my mother's room, her gentle, drug-induced snores sounding like prayer bells. The women watched as their movers hauled mattresses and vanities, potted plants and marked boxes in through the front door. I wondered if they knew the truth about this place, about the man who swung from their rafters and the ghost of a family buried in the yard across the street.

Mostly, I wondered what they were like. The old woman stood on the front porch smoking a cigar, craning her clouded, sightless eyes up to the window where I watched, as though she could smell me. Behind her, the daughter loitered in the open doorway, leering at the moving guys, her crop top barely covering the underside of breasts far more developed than my own. And the mother failed to notice or care. She smiled, the look radiant and full of an eastern wind that had long since drifted from our sails. What was it like to smile in the face of tragedy? To look at the wreckage and see…possibility?

As dusk fell and our new neighbors tipped the moving guys, I let the curtains drop closed and skirted the edge of my mother's bed, pulling open the door to the closet as silently as I could. If I pushed her slacks back, I could just make out the pale blue of Robby's old walls. Mom moved into his room three weeks after the funeral, after they'd boxed up all his old things and called in a crew to repaint. She and Dad hadn't shared a bed since.

In the beginning, the dead are always with you. It's almost as if they aren't even gone, as though you could round any given corner and see them there, waiting. For months after Robby died, I heard his voice, his laughter catching in his throat, the sound of his footfalls down the long hall upstairs. I could feel his towheaded locks soft against the pads of my fingers still and imagine his quiet breathing in the night. It was all there, floating around me, able to be summoned forward at any given moment. Like a balloon, I had Robby's memory, his soul, on a string.

But that only lasts as long as the pain is fresh. You bleed memories for a while. And then one day you find you've bled them all out. And the sharp sting of loss has waned into a dull ache.

It's the little things that go first. The way light would play across his face at a certain angle. The expression he made when he pouted. The smell of him in the morning. You go to summon some detail up from the depths and it's no longer there. The dead drift away.

And then even the dull ache disappears, and only numbness holds in its place. You stop trying to recall details because the futility of it is worse than the grief. It's no longer the loss of the person you mourn, but the loss of the haunt. And the absence is all that is left when you reach for your pain.

I suppose this is what they mean when they say, "Life goes on." But it's no kind of life. And my parents and I hardly qualified as living. Something presses forward. Some motor that won't stop running. Like automatons, we marched through an endless parade of days. We drank coffee and got the mail.

We went to our respective cells: the office, the boardroom, the school bus. We kept breathing and talking and eating and beating. But we stopped living the day Robby died. That's the secret no one knows. No one outside of this house anyway. We all died that day, in the pool in the yard. We were buried, and filled in, and covered up, and forgotten. We were lost. And we've been dead ever since.

I let my fingers trace over the last remnants of a brother I was to pretend I never had. Robby. *My little boy blue.* He was the only person I could talk to anymore. And he was dead. It didn't say much for us as a family. In the closet, I thought I could even still smell the scent of him—sunshine and baby shampoo and little boy sweat.

"We're not alone anymore, Robby," I told him before putting myself to bed that night. I could still see the orange glow of the grandma's cigar burning from the porch across the way through my window.

CHAPTER 2

Everything started the morning after they moved in. It began in a small way, like white noise. An indecipherable hum rising from the lifeless pit of our existence. I might have recognized it as I was making my toast in the kitchen had I not been dead myself. I might have known when Dad shuffled in, his dress shirt rumpled and black moons cradling his eyes. He'd just gotten the coffeepot going when Mom wafted down, her silk robe trailing like ether behind her. We were all answering the call—*their* call, the mysterious bell that was sounding in the hollows of our hearts, high and silent, like a dog whistle.

The kitchen felt small with all of us in it, crowded by our thoughts. The table was no better. For every full seat, there would always be the empty one. We sat in awkward silence, pretending this was normal—that *we* were normal. But we hadn't spent a morning together in years.

My toast broke against the pressure of the butter knife, and

I pushed the plate away. "We have new neighbors."

My dad put down his iPad and glanced up at me over his steaming cup. "What was that?"

My mom lifted weary eyes.

"New neighbors. The people across the street moved in… yesterday."

"Oh. I didn't realize that house had sold." He looked wobbly under the weight of conversation.

"Last month," I said.

Mom knew, but she hadn't told him. It proved how little they spoke anymore.

"Did you see them?" she asked, her voice rough and thick against the pull of the drugs in her system.

I nodded.

"And?" Dad said, his eyes rising to the window behind my chair, the one that overlooked the street, searching.

I shrugged. "They're women."

"Lesbians?" Something flashed behind my mother's heavy gaze, something akin to alertness, to sanity, but falling sadly short.

"A family, I think—a girl and her mother and grandmother."

My dad studied the window behind me, the sunlight highlighting all the quiet years on his face. We wouldn't talk about yesterday, Robby's death day. We never did. We wouldn't look at the empty chair at the end of the table or ask one another how we were coping. This *was* coping, this disregard, this surrender to finality.

"We should take them something," Dad said at last. He looked at my mother. "Rita, *you* should take them something.

Welcome them to the neighborhood. It's the least we can do for them for buying that eyesore of a house."

Mom gathered her robe into a fist in front of her chest, a look of alarm spreading across her features like ice melt. "I–I couldn't possibly. Goddammit, Richard, you know I…This is no time…Olivia can do it."

My father turned to me, his face resigned. I looked to my mother, and her eyes found my own, full of pleading, then commanding, then empty again.

"Yeah, I guess," I said. What else could I say? I'd grown accustomed in the last few years to this kind of responsibility, shielding them from the living. I answered the door whenever someone knocked. I signed one of their names to my own report cards. I made excuses when they missed something at my school, ran to the drugstore to drop Mom's prescriptions off, and called for pizza or Chinese takeout whenever Dad came home hungry. This was my new role. I was the ambassador to what had once been the Foster family.

"Fine. I'll pick something up and drop it off for you before I leave for the office."

I nodded my assent.

"I'm going upstairs," my mother said, rising from the table. She looked pale in the light.

I watched her walk away with a kind of wistfulness, remembering the big Saturday breakfasts she used to cook in that robe. The smell of eggs and melted butter filled my nose for a split second and then faded. I looked at my broken toast.

"I'm going to shower," Dad said, scooting his chair back. "Thanks, kiddo," he added, giving my shoulder a small pat.

He left the room, and I sat at our table alone, remembering what it felt like to be us before the fall.

The potted calla lily in my hands looked too perfect to be real. I found it sitting on the kitchen counter when I came back down after getting dressed. My dad was already gone. In his place, this ghostly white flower waited for me, its yellow tongue mute and protruding. I stood on our front step staring at it for a moment before I recalled myself and my task and began the journey forward.

The sun was high, and my shadow crept ahead of me, touching everything a moment before I could. The street felt wider than I remembered; the house, taller. A dry, brown lawn received me, a wide front porch. Its gray-blue paint was peeling away under the strain of neglect and summer heat. The old woman sat in a rocker near the front door. I climbed the three steps and stood before her, but her hazy eyes, which had found me the night before from across the asphalt, now stared at some phantom point in the distance, unseeing.

My shadow lay over her like a dark blanket. I stretched my lips in the semblance of a smile and looked down, but she continued her fragile rocking, her distant stare. I held the potted flower out to her. I waited. My mouth grew dry with the stale greeting trapped in it.

At last, I said, "Hi."

She did not budge. Didn't lift a lash. Was she deaf too?

"Hello?" I tried again. "I'm Olivia, from across the street. I brought you something to welcome you to the neighborhood." My arms stiffened before her, the trembling lily hanging between us like a wintry breath.

She neither saw my gesture nor heard my words. Confused, paralyzed by this cleft in social niceties, I stood silently for a moment. I let my eyes travel over my shoulder in the direction her gaze was pinned, but I saw nothing to catch my interest. Yards. Houses. Trees. Mailboxes. A blue Chevy parked on the curb. An orange tomcat sidling between its tires. Frustrated, I turned back and knelt down. Perhaps if I looked *up* at her...

The screech of the screen door sent me tumbling backward onto my rear, but I managed to hold the plant steady. Above me towered a large woman with a mane of red hair flowing over her shoulders. The mother. Her pink face lit with a grand smile as she reached down to help me up. "You must be our neighbor!" she said delightedly.

I dusted my ass with one hand and pushed the plant at her. "Yes. My mother sent this over. She'd come herself, but she's not feeling well."

Everyone on our street knew better than to expect anything from Rita Foster. She hadn't felt well in three years. Her addiction was the Voldemort of the neighborhood—dare not name it for what it was. So there was something refreshing in the ignorance of this exchange. I didn't have to cut my gaze away as I told the familiar lie. I didn't have to stand shrinking under her unspoken judgment. There wasn't any.

The woman's skin was tan with years of trapped sun and her eyes were blue as a jay's wing. They flickered to our house and back to me. Her smile fell momentarily. "Poor dear," she said. "You must come inside and let me give you something for her."

I tensed. *Inside?* Inside was not part of the deal. "Oh, no. I couldn't. I..." I sounded just like my mother at the table this morning. My stomach turned on the realization. "Sure," I agreed, deflated.

"You must excuse my mother. She's older than Methuselah and exceedingly blind," the woman told me as she took my elbow. "*And even more stubborn*," she added into my ear.

At this, the old woman seemed to shake from her reverie. Her face rose. Her eyes rose. And then she rose to her full height before us. Suddenly, her milky eyes found mine with no delay, settling over me with all the warmth of the grave. "I hear just fine," she said as she turned away and scooted toward the door.

My breath stuck in my throat. I felt five years old again, sitting before the principal's desk at school, having been overheard calling my teacher the *b* word. I was too young to know what I was saying, but I'd heard my dad call my mom that word the night before as they fought over some unknown cause doing the dishes after dinner. They used to fight regularly. It was never serious. Even as a child I knew not to fear it. It was the friction of so much charge pouring off both of them—live wires as they were. A way to release the static. I missed those fights now.

The woman rubbed at my shoulder after her mother had disappeared inside. "You see?" she said jovially.

But the old woman's remark had ignited something within me. Something deep. Something I hadn't actually felt in three years, since the worst of it had been realized—fear.

The woman held the screen door open for me. "I'm Rhea. You must come in, Olivia," she said warmly.

I stepped over the threshold, struck by an unsettling thought. Had I told her my name?

CHAPTER 3

Rhea breezed past me toward an open doorway to the right of the stairs.

"Where are you from?" I asked, shaking off the strange feeling.

"Pennsylvania," she called back.

I stepped past a formal living room to my left. It was still all boxed up except for an antique armchair and a smoking table. It was here the old woman had resettled her bones, a fat cigar poised between her papery lips as she held a lit match to one end and puffed as though it were her last breath.

She ignored me, and I continued toward the infamous stairwell I'd climbed so many times as a child. The air hung differently in here. Windows were open all around to ventilate the house, but something tangible remained. It was like walking through a spiderweb. I could feel the invisible threads of this house, these women, clinging to me, but I couldn't see to tear them off.

The stairwell was unchanged, the faded brown carpet running over it like pet fur. The banister was still dingy with the little fingers that had once gripped it, but something had chased the gloom away. The distraught dad who had taken his own life no longer filled the space at the top of the landing. My fear of him had nowhere to place itself—something new haunted the stairway now. A shadow flitted above.

A soft sound filtered down the stairs. Singing.

I was rapt by her voice, by the lightness of it. It sounded like freedom, like fresh rain and fireflies. Like something I once remembered and had forgotten. I moved, trancelike, toward it. But just before I could ascend the stairs, Rhea's voice called my attention through the open doorway to the kitchen, where she was bustling about.

"Hallas."

"Pardon?" I blinked and moved away from the stairs and into the kitchen, baptized in the light of the half a dozen fluorescent bulbs overhead.

Rhea looked up from the fridge. "Hallas. It's our last name. You were wondering, weren't you?"

"I guess," I said. Had I been? I turned back to look toward the stairs, but the singing had died away and, with it, my curiosity.

"Yours?" she questioned, her bright eyes lighting on me for a moment.

"Foster," I told her. "We live across the street."

Rhea smiled. "I know. I saw your dad leaving for work this morning. Or is he your stepdad?"

I took a seat on a barstool at the high counter. He wasn't

my stepdad, but he wasn't my dad anymore. What could I call him? A shade. He was the shade of my dad. "No."

Rhea nodded. "It's good to hear about a couple who's not divorced for a change." She handed me an open soda.

"Are you? Divorced?" I sipped my soda loudly. It tasted sweeter here than it did at home. There was an intensity to everything these women touched.

She laughed. "Oh no! Never married. Kara's dad is…well, it's easiest to just say he's gone. It's only us and my mother, Sybil."

"Kara?" I could almost hear the singing echo in my chest cavity, between my ears.

"My daughter. She's upstairs now, but she'll be down later. You should meet her. You'd like each other, I think."

Yes. The girl in the doorway. The one with the cutoffs and the large breasts. The one the moving men ogled like they hadn't had a drink in a year and she was iced tea. She was the singer on the stairs. The disembodied voice. But she was nothing like me. She was alive. And I had little to interest anyone except the morose.

"I should go," I said suddenly, jumping up.

"Are you sure?" Rhea asked.

"Yes. I forgot that my mom needs me to do some chores." I backed toward the kitchen doorway, away from Rhea's broad smile and ruddy cheeks and flaming hair. She was too alive to be real. Like the daughter. Like the calla lily.

"Here! Take this," she offered, thrusting a jar out in one hand. I took it in my own without a second glance and backed out of the kitchen. Turning, I saw the potted lily I had brought on an end table by the stair banister.

The flower, which had been milky white before, was suddenly now a livid, bleeding red.

My mouth dropped open and I bolted for the door. Past the haunted stairs. Past the smoking grandmother. Past the creepy porch with peeling paint. I was across the street and in my own house, my back against the door, my heart flopping in my chest like a fish out of its bowl, before I looked down at the jar in my hands.

Pomegranate Jelly the label read in simple script. So innocuous, but I felt as if I were holding one of those specimen jars with organs floating in formaldehyde.

I caught my breath and placed a hand over my thumping heart, willing it to behave. I looked at the jar again and almost laughed. Obviously, I'd confused our plant with one they already had. Probably one another neighbor had brought over. But this explanation couldn't quite reach the undercurrent of fear still moving inside me. It had to be that house. Something about it still unsettled me after all these years. Because a houseplant, a jar of jelly, and an old woman weren't reasonable things to be afraid of.

So why did I feel like an open wound?

Sometimes, I tell myself the story of my own life. When I wake at night and the dawn shadows are summoned from beyond the horizon, I put myself back to sleep with these stories. There are a multitude of ways to render the story that is *me*. In some versions, Robby was never born. And the unborn cannot die. In these versions, we don't miss his downy hair or lopsided smile. We never had a pool...or a boy. There is just me, my parents, and a stream of days in which we are infinitely content. In these versions, I am free to live the life I once imagined for myself. I go to college. I marry my first love. I make art. My life follows a well-established rhythm that has been laid out for it. I am normal, unmarked by tragedy.

In other versions, Robby comes and goes. He blooms, ripens, and withers on the vine. He graduates. He dates. He drives a car and says things like "no kidding?" and "good grief." He grows, marries, and has his own children. He stands beside me at our parents' funerals. He is unblemished. He is real. He is alive. And I am much the same as before. I draw constantly. I read incessantly. I fall in love too easily. Still, I am normal. *We* are normal. I delight in being a *we*. I take it for granted.

But my favorite stories are the ones where Robby toddles to the pool's edge, and I am lying in the sun in my first bikini. I see him approach and feel the fine hairs along my arms rise in warning. I jump up and plunge into the water just as he topples over. I come up choking and gasping, Robby crying in my arms. I save the day. Not just *the* day—every day. I save the countless possible days that Robby would otherwise never know. I am not normal in this story. I am better than normal. I am heroic.

The story I am trapped in doesn't end like these. It never crests, crescendos, peaks, and dips back down into a resolution we can settle happily into. Instead it slithers, bucks, and then slides along, dragging us with it. We are a snag in life. We live in its wake. Our rhythm is out of sync. Normal is a thing of the past, and I am the opposite of a hero.

I don't draw anymore. Inspiration has left the building. My sketchbooks and pencils collect dust on a darkened shelf in my closet. I can't read, can't follow a sentence without realizing I've lost track of its meaning by the time I meet the first bit of punctuation. My books have all been donated to the local library.

I don't love. My heart is missing a vital piece, and it's hard to fall when you're already lying at rock bottom.

The night after I met Rhea Hallas, I must have told myself a dozen of these stories. Nothing sufficed. Nothing drove away the stain of the lily or the sound of singing. In my mind, I just kept climbing those stairs, rising…rising…

I sat up in bed and threw my blankets back. My room was cast in shades of gray from the streetlamp outside. The shadows gave everything a transient feeling, as though somehow the very substance of things was just an illusion. I lowered my feet to the floor, half expecting them to disappear into the carpet but was greeted by soft piling and a firm reality check. Everything was still here, even if every*one* was not.

Downstairs, the house swam in the shadows. No one had bothered to close the blinds before going to bed. The kitchen appliances held a dull gleam in the cast of the streetlights. On the counter, the light caught the angles of a single diamond-textured jar. Ms. Hallas's jelly.

In the gray twilight of our home, the jar of jelly gleamed like a multifaceted ruby. It glowed with ethereal light, a brazen beacon calling me down from my nightly reveries. The jar and I were connected. Nocturnal. While our neighbors slept, tucked under their matching linen duvets in their matching brick-and-mortar houses all along the street, we two were haunted.

I moved soundlessly through the kitchen and wrapped my fingers around the cool glass. The jelly's garish glow mimicked the lily I'd seen in the Hallases' home. A vulgar, sensual thing that didn't belong. Not in my world. I was simultaneously drawn and repelled by it. Just as I was with the Hallases themselves, as I'd always been to that house.

The lid popped off with a couple of turns. In the still silence of our home, the hushed scraping sound of metal against glass as it parted was so loud it could have been a rooster's crow. My body flooded with recognition at the scent of sunshine, dry earth, and Mediterranean salt water. I turned and leaned against the counter and simply stood there, holding the jar, breathing in deeper and deeper. I had never encountered anything so alluring. Not even the memory of Prescott Peters washing his dad's car with no shirt on last summer compared. And that had been about as close to hunger as I'd been in the last three years.

My heart hammered, my lungs ached to taste more, and my mouth watered, but the overload of my senses was too horrific to bear. Like those moments in time when you become terribly present, when everything slams into place around you and the absolute awareness that there is nothing beyond this one horrible moment invades your mind with deafening accuracy. Those moments are rarely ever good ones. They are the crises we encounter. The proverbial flash of life before the eyes. The ambulance sirens and the flashing lights. The second before impact. The stillness in the storm.

I slammed the lid back onto the jar and screwed it shut, leaving it on the counter and backing away from it with shaking hands. Whatever was in that jelly, I wanted no part of it. What did they preserve the fruit with anyway? How could you take a deliriously warm afternoon in Cyprus, with the dust on your feet and an umbrella of azure sky overhead, and lock it away in a jar?

I kept backing up until I bumped into our dining table. And then I stood there watching the jar watch me—a great, red eye. My fear exploded, and I spun away, unable to look at it any longer.

Through the darkness outside of our window, I saw the orange gleam of lit tobacco staring from across the street. I was caught between the eyes of a beast I didn't understand, and there was nowhere to hide anymore.

CHAPTER 4

The door made a muffled click behind me as I braced my fingers against it to slow the close. I wrapped my arms around my chest and stepped forward out of the shadows of our front stoop and into the streetlamp. I watched the slow burn of the old woman's cigar in the night fade in and out with her inhales, a heartbeat all its own. It had to be after 2:00 a.m. There were no cars. No neighbors out walking their dogs or getting their papers. It was just she and I and the stars overhead.

I crossed their yard without looking up and climbed the steps of their porch until I stood before her rocking chair, mute and seeking. Her cloudy eyes didn't even wiggle in their sockets to acknowledge me, but I knew she sensed me just the same.

She took a long drag of her cigar and let it out with the kind of tender attentiveness old men reserved for their whiskey. And then she let her hand rest on the weathered arm of the chair, and her face looked out over the domestic calm of our street as though she were looking across the ocean.

"Did you eat it?" she asked at last.

I stood, rooted before her, my robe dancing around my calves in the rare night breeze. Even without the sun, the tyranny of the drought was palpable. "What?"

"Did. You. Eat. It." She took another drag of her cigar.

I watched her wrinkled lips pucker around it, then relax and release. There was such rhythm in the gesture, such care. A mother kissing her child's brow. It was mesmerizing.

"No." I looked back at our house from the Hallases' porch. Crisp, white HardiePlank, black shutters, painted brick. Even from here, I could see the red throb of jelly through the window.

Her face turned up to mine, her eyes searching for something they shouldn't be able to find. She had an accent I couldn't place. Her grizzled hair hung in silver threads around her shoulders. Her hand reached out for mine, bulbous knuckles and aged skin, knotty as an ancient oak. But her fingers were so cold to the touch.

"I'll tell you a story."

"Pardon?"

"Sit."

I obeyed her, though I couldn't say why. I folded my legs against the dry boards of the porch at her feet and waited for her to begin.

"The day Kara was born—Kara, my granddaughter, you'll meet her soon. The day Kara was born, my mother died."

My mind tripped over the math. This woman looked to be in her eighties, but it was late, I was tired, and her voice was like slowly tearing paper. I never had a head for figures.

"My heart has never been so full and so empty at the same

time. I didn't know the human heart could do that, but it can. It can hold two things at once, like two hands. In one day, my heart split. One half held the ashes of my mother's life like an urn, the other cradled the squirming, newborn body of my granddaughter. In that moment, I went blind. True story. I looked on Kara once and one time only. But I've learned to see many things without my vision. I see you."

She put the cigar to her lips and inhaled slowly, waiting for me to respond.

I wasn't sure what to say, so I said nothing.

Smoke furled from between her lips. Her hand tightened around my own. "When we try to hold on to the dead, we lose pieces of ourselves."

She took another drag. "Not all in a rush, no. Gradually, like leaves falling from a tree. First one, then another. It's a measured disintegration. The only way to stop it is to let go. Most never realize it's happening at all."

I got clumsily to my feet. I wasn't sure I wanted this old woman seeing any more of me tonight.

"You come back tomorrow," she said.

I swallowed. "Why?" My voice was a cracked whisper.

"You come back tomorrow." She dropped my hand and rose from her chair, disappearing into the house behind the screen door, leaving me on their porch.

I sat on the steps alone and looked at our house. The live oak that had crowned our yard with its deciduous glory year after year seemed sad in its lonely post. The drought was taking its toll. That tree had stood proud for over a hundred years, and now, in a single summer, it might be wiped from the earth. Something about its cruel story resonated deep in me. The fragility of life. Robby's. The tree's. Ours. Mine.

My eyes traveled up to the window that was my room, vacant now. I didn't feel the tears at first, had no idea they were falling. It was the wetness of my pajama leg against my knee that alerted me at all. But I wasn't crying for Robby. Not this time. I was crying for the girl who used to live in that room. The girl who had nurtured a secret crush on Prescott Peters since second grade, who ate paste when someone dared her to, who chewed gum and doodled stars on the corners of her homework. The girl who passed notes to Mia Perez every time a teacher's back was turned until Mia moved away four years ago. The girl who loved to draw so much she carried a sketchbook with her everywhere, who lived vicariously through the fictional lives and loves of her favorite YA characters, who couldn't dance or catch a ball to save her life, but who could name all fifty states and their capitals, make the meanest peanut-butter-and-banana sandwich this side of the Mississippi, and say *I love you* in seven languages.

And now, sitting across the street on the front porch of our new neighbors' house, it seemed so far away. Like a movie seen once, something flat and purely entertaining—a romantic comedy. It was bright and flashy and larger than life at the time. It filled the audience with hope and laughter and the belief in tomorrow. And it was simply over. The screen was blank. The audience was gone. The theater was empty. But knowing it wasn't real didn't take away the longing for it to be.

It was a silly, girlish life, but it had been mine. It had been enough. How many pieces of myself had I lost already?

CHAPTER 5

I didn't go back the next day. Or the next. Or the next. I had no intention of going back at all. Whatever the Hallases were about, I decided I wanted no part of it. At night I rose from my bed, went downstairs, and threw the jar of pomegranate jelly in the trash bin. And every morning I awoke, stumbled down the steps, and found it impossibly back on the counter, taunting me.

Until the morning it wasn't.

A week must have passed since I'd sat at the old woman's feet and listened to her bizarre story. I woke early, too early. It was only just past dawn. But a vivid sunrise seemed to burn through the dark of my sleeping mind and tear me to consciousness. I went downstairs thinking I'd get a glass of water, maybe tea, maybe cereal. Something to fill me up inside, to weigh me down.

The kitchen light was on. My mother was at the table, her back to me, in a faded Unity Realty T-shirt and matted hair.

For the first time since I brought it home, the counter was empty of Ms. Hallas's jar of jelly. But my stomach twisted on itself, disbelieving.

I opened the pantry door and looked into the trash bin. Empty.

I looked over at my mother and the table before her. There sat the open jar, a salad plate, a slice of white bread, and a knife. Smeared across the half-toasted bread slice was pomegranate jelly and butter. I should have been happy to find her awake, to see her eating. But a surge of panic crested in me, and I lunged for the table, swiping at the jar and her plate.

"Jesus, Olivia! What's gotten into you?" My mother jumped up and stared at me with wide eyes.

I couldn't answer. Why didn't I treat her pill bottles that way? "I don't want you eating this."

Her eyes narrowed into a drug-fueled glare. Hate burned behind them. It used to frighten me—now it excited me. Anger was something. It meant she was still alive in there. "Give it back, Olivia. I don't care what you want."

"No." I stepped toward the pantry where the open trash was waiting.

"I said give it back! I'm still your mother."

I leveled my gaze on her. "Could've fooled me."

At that she lunged forward, swiping at me. The plate dropped and shattered across the floor, but her hands clamped around the open jar I still held. "You little bitch!" she shrieked. "Give it back!"

If I could have stepped outside of myself and looked back at us, I would have stopped. I don't know why I was fighting or what for. It was just a jar of jelly. She had a dozen prescription bottles that were a thousand times more damaging than Ms. Hallas's homemade jam. But I was trapped in the peculiarities and dysfunction of my world. I was as blind as the old woman across the street. I couldn't see my mother anymore. I couldn't see myself.

Her slender fingers were weak at best and they shook. I was stronger than she was, steadier. I managed to rip the jar from her grasp only to lose my own hold on it. It sailed away from both of us, smashing against the kitchen tile, exploding into bits of glass and bloodlike splatters.

But her hands were on me now, her fingers tangling in my hair, her shrieks maddening in my ears. "Why? Why?" she screamed over and over as I grappled with her, swatting at her arms, trying to pull away as she shook my head between her hands. "Give him back! Give him back, you bitch!"

I lost all sense of reason. I didn't know who we were. I didn't know where or why. I simply wanted to get away. I dug my nails into anything they came into contact with and howled at the top of my lungs for help.

When something at last came between us, Mom tore away from me with fistfuls of my hair in her hands, her eyes blood red with manic rage. My dad held her in his arms as she reached for me, grinding her teeth, until the screams became sobs, and the sobs became wails, and the wails became shudders.

He looked at me, all business. "Olivia, upstairs. Get the Xanax bottle. It's next to the alarm clock. Quickly!"

I was halfway up the staircase before I realized I'd been crying too. But there was no time to comfort myself. We had to put the beast back in its cage.

Back downstairs, I passed Dad the bottle with shaky hands.

"Water," he commanded.

I handed him a half-full glass as he pressed a tablet past her cracked lips. "Drink, Rita," he said, pushing the rim of the cup against her mouth. She tried to spit the pill back out, to push it away with her tongue, but he was holding her strongly with one arm and tipping the glass back with another. She choked and sputtered for a second, but she finally swallowed and the pill went down.

I took the glass and backed away, my dad smoothing the wild hair around her face. His eyes surveyed the room, the minefield of broken glass and slippery mush. He took her hands in his, pulling my hair from them, dropping it to the floor with the rest of the mess. "I'm taking her upstairs," he said, not quite meeting my eyes. "Clean this up."

It took me nearly an hour to find and wipe the specks of red from every last surface. I crept back up the stairs when I was done, past the soft snoring of my mother's room, and curled up on my own bed. This *eruption* had been three years coming. It wasn't the jar of jelly that had pushed her over the edge. She didn't usually say it, but she didn't have to. I saw it in the slant of her gaze and the tight lines around her mouth and the way she resisted touching me. I knew part of my mother would always blame me for Robby's death. And I couldn't even fault her for it because I blamed myself.

By now, morning was in full swing. I lay there listening to the sounds of my dad getting ready for work. I waited until I heard the door close, the garage open, the car drive away.

I slunk into my mother's room, watching the rise and fall of her chest as I pilfered through the assortment of bottles on her nightstand. Finding the Ambien, I quickly popped one, washing it down with the mixture of flat Sprite and melted ice that was left over from the night before, and returned to my room, locking the door behind me.

I'd been helping myself to her stash for the last eight months, but only when the situation called for it. I'd even begun stockpiling my own secret assortment of pills in nooks and crannies around my room for those times when I couldn't get them directly from the bottle for one reason or another—Xanax in the makeup bag in the bottom drawer, Wellbutrin under the mattress, hydrocodone in the empty laptop case. After this morning's breakdown, I'd earned myself a little oblivion. I didn't want to die. I didn't even want to check out. I just wanted to sleep and forget.

I watched the curtains over my window until the shadows began bleeding into one another, forming shapes and faces in the light that tried in vain to break into the crypt that was our house. I saw Robby's softly rounded head in a fold of the fabric, and the smoke from the old woman's cigar dancing. I saw my own dark hair hanging from my mother's clenched fingers. I saw the splatter pattern of Ms. Hallas's jelly on our tile floor. I saw the grim reaper, sickle over one shoulder, and Prescott Peters bending over his car, and the stars I used to doodle on my notebook. And then, finally, *gratefully*, I slept, and I saw nothing anymore.

CHAPTER 6

When I woke up, it was a quarter after four in the afternoon. My dad would be home in a few hours. He was good on the days when Mom flipped out. He came home from work. He sat in the living room and pretended to watch TV. Sometimes he even made dinner. It was almost comforting.

I scrubbed my face and brushed my teeth and put some clothes on. I had decided to take a walk. I didn't know why, except that I didn't want to be alone here with Mom anymore, with her accusations ringing in my ears. I tied on my sneakers and stepped outside, not bothering to lock the front door. I'd no sooner made it down the sidewalk than the sound of a voice arrested me.

"Hey!" A curvy adolescent girl bound down the front steps of the Hallases' porch and stalked toward me. "You're Olivia, right?"

The girl from moving day stood before me, the singer on the stairs. She was clad in cutoffs and a black camisole. Barefoot, her toes were painted pink with little skulls and crossbones on each one. She wore a long chain with a crooked-arrow pendant at the end. Her mess of wavy, blond hair was cropped at her shoulders, the roots dark. Smudged eyeliner underlined her blue-gray eyes. Her face was focused on mine, intent. The weight of her stare was disproportionate to her age.

"Yeah. I live across the street."

"I know," she said dully. "I just saw you come out."

"Right." I glanced away and back again, but her eyes never wavered. "I was just going to take a walk."

"Cool," she replied. "I'll come with."

I wanted to be alone, but I couldn't see telling her that. I waited a moment, expecting her to go back for her shoes, but she just stared at me.

"Well, start walking already."

"Oh. Uh, don't you need your shoes?"

She looked down, wiggling her pink toes with their little symbols of death. "Why?"

I sighed and started slowly down the street, remembering what it felt like to pick splinters of glass out of my heels this morning. Fortunately, none of them had been deep or very large.

"I'm Kara," she said after a few moments. "My mom said you're the same age as me."

I didn't remember telling Rhea Hallas how old I was, but maybe I had. Kara and I were two opposite poles of the teen spectrum. I seemed to be developing a little behind the curve, and she seemed to be developing a little ahead of it. I found it hard to believe we would be in the same grade. "I guess. I'm sixteen."

"Do you have your license yet?"

"Just last month." I took an after-school driver's education course that met in the tech class in the back of our school. I drove myself to get my license when it was over, my dad dozing in the passenger seat. I hadn't driven much since then though. "You?"

"Nope. Just a learner's permit. Moving kind of threw everything off."

I nodded.

"So what does everyone do around here? For fun?"

I crossed my arms over my chest. I didn't know. Fun wasn't in my repertoire anymore. I had friends once. Maybe not like Kara, but girls who cared about things like nail polish and what movies were playing at the mall. Girls who giggled and shrieked and whispered behind backs. Girls who knew how to have fun. Those girls left me in the dust after Robby died, when *fun* moved beyond my reach. They whispered about me now and giggled when they thought I couldn't hear. I shrugged and made a noncommittal noise.

Kara seemed unhindered. She reached into a pocket of her practically nonexistent shorts and pulled out a sucker, like the kind they give you at the doctor's office after getting your shots. She held it out to me, but I shook my head. Within a heartbeat, she'd unwrapped it and popped it into her mouth. "You know some guy hung himself in our house?" she said around the lollipop.

I looked up to see her smiling, a bulge in one cheek, her face awash with dark fascination.

"Yeah. I know. It was a long time ago." I tried to focus back on the street.

Her eyes went far away, like she was considering something. We walked for a few long moments like that—me, Kara, the lollipop, and her thinking so loud it was practically audible. My sneakers thudded against the pavement. Kara's feet were black underneath when she'd lift them to take another step. Everything about her was the opposite of subtle.

Finally, she plucked the candy from her mouth and held a hand out to stop me. Already, her tongue was turning a vulgar crimson. "What was it like?"

"When Mr. Dearing hung himself?" Was she serious? "I don't know. Tragic?"

Kara's face was sharp in the afternoon sun, her long lashes glinting in the golden light, her eyes boring into mine without reprieve. "No. When your brother died."

I wanted to be angry—should have been. It was rude, too personal, sensational. But it was also the most honest, most direct thing anyone had said to me since Robby's funeral. It was the only real conversation I was capable of having. Everything else was a script.

"You know when you're awake really early in the morning and it's just before dawn? And for a few moments, everything gets really, really still and really, really quiet, like the whole world is holding its breath for the sunrise?"

Kara nodded.

"It was like that. Only the sun never rose."

She took a step toward me on the street, overwhelming my senses. Suddenly, I was aware of her knockoff perfume and the cherry smell of her sucker, the red stain forming between her lips where it had been moments before—the devastating presence of her filled up the spaces around and inside me.

"Are you still doing it?" she asked.

I was paralyzed by her gaze, the heat emanating from her skin, her fascination with me. "What?"

"Holding your breath?"

In that moment, I exhaled.

Before I could respond, a voice called my name from behind, and Kara's heady gaze loosened, shifted, and refocused somewhere behind me.

Just like that, her spell was broken.

I spun around to see Prescott Peters poised in his driveway, a basketball tucked under one arm, a dimple showing in one cheek. I hadn't realized we'd walked so far.

Kara stepped around me to move toward him, her hand catching my wrist and tugging me along. I followed like an obedient shadow, watching a ripple of energy make its way up her form.

He smiled at me as we approached, but I was fairly certain he was more interested in meeting Kara than in finding out how I'd been. We grew up together, played hide-and-seek and a dozen different versions of tag when we were little, caught snails and traded ghost stories, made s'mores in his backyard, and slept on his trampoline in thin, pink-and-green sleeping bags on summer nights. He was my best friend without ever having to say it out loud, but somewhere around junior high, I began to develop an awareness of Prescott that made casual encounters all but impossible. As had nearly every other girl at our school.

And then Robby died. And Prescott became mythic in my

mind, synonymous with everything I ever wanted but could never have again.

"Haven't seen you on this end of the street in a long time," he said. He didn't mean it, didn't realize what he was saying, but I kind of hated him for it anyway, for the aloof, untouchable way other people appeared to go on with their lives while I was standing still.

Kara's appraising smile didn't falter, but she seemed to register my discomfort, the trip in my heart rate. She stepped nearer to me, but her eyes never left Prescott's. "I'm Olivia's new neighbor."

"Prescott, this is Kara," I said flatly. Introductions done, my part was now obsolete. I could disappear into the pavement again, forget the last time I stood at the end of Prescott's driveway. It couldn't have been more than a few days before Robby's death.

"Hey," he said. "Guess we're neighbors too."

Kara shrugged one shoulder. "Guess so."

"I'm gonna head back," I said, trying to squirm out from between the onslaught of hormones I was caught between.

Kara looped an arm in mine. "Olivia's going to take me out driving to see the area tomorrow. Wanna come?"

"Sure." Prescott beamed. Both dimples were on display now, like bookends for his perfect row of teeth.

My mouth fell open, but I could barely comprehend what I'd heard, let alone form a response. "I–I don't think my mom will let me take her car," I said lamely, though everyone on the block likely knew my mother wouldn't stop drooling long enough to notice it or I was gone.

Prescott didn't miss a beat. He shifted the basketball to the other arm. "We can use mine. Just come knock when you're ready to go."

"Perfect! See you tomorrow," Kara called as I unfolded my arm from hers, ducked my head, and began briskly walking away.

"Hold up," she said a few houses down, tugging on me until I slowed. "Olivia, what's wrong? I thought you liked him."

I glared at her. "I never said I'd take you anywhere."

She crossed her arms and looked at me skeptically. "You got big plans?"

"No, but—"

"So," she said with a shrug, "now you do."

"You don't understand."

"What's to understand? You like him. You were just too scared to do anything about it on your own."

"I don't like Prescott. Sure, he's attractive. But I can't be around him."

Kara looked smug. "And why not?"

Because I was talking to Prescott when Robby fell into our pool and drowned. I couldn't say it of course. To say that out loud was to voice the guilt that had gnawed at my edges each and every day for the last three years. It was to give it life and form and permission to do what it wanted. And that was the equivalent of lying down in front of a runaway train. "Never mind. I'll go. But just tomorrow."

Kara grinned the way I imagine a stray cat would if it spotted a baby bird fallen from the nest. "I'll come for you around noon."

CHAPTER 7

I am a dead girl.

I had never been more sure of that realization than after meeting Kara Hallas face-to-face. Nor had I cared. It seemed I cared about nothing until the Hallases showed up. And then, I cared about all the wrong things, like that stupid pomegranate jelly and the old woman seeing me—seeing *into* me. And the lilt and lift of Kara's voice that didn't match the curve of her figure or the heft of her stare.

Right now, I cared about what jeans I was going to wear, or if my hair was clean enough, or if I could stand next to Prescott Peters all day without making sweat rings under my sleeves. And all of this care felt stiff as old used Kleenex in my heart. Part of me hated it. Part of me hoped it—hoped Kara—would never leave.

My teeth were flossed. My hair was combed. I'd even dabbed on a little makeup, but not much. Just enough to cover the permanent bruise-colored rings that had lodged themselves beneath my eyes. My dad was at work.

The night before, he'd found me heating up a pack of instant macaroni and stood, hands on hips, heaving a resigned sigh. I waited for the words that would follow. "Olivia…your mother…About this morning…"

"Dad, it's okay. I know." I stirred noodles and avoided eye contact.

"It's best if we don't antagonize her. Not right now. Not until she gets over this…bump."

"Right. I know. I'm sorry."

He left the kitchen, giving me a quick pat on the back.

And that was it. He always referred to her addiction that way. It was a bump or a hill or a phase. Something small and rounded—a decipherable, measurable curve we could track her progress by. Something with an up, a peak, and a down. But I'd lost track of her position over the last three years. She never peaked, never came down. We were always just climbing, climbing to some legendary summit lost among the clouds. One that I doubted even existed. She was Sisyphus incarnate, rolling her pain uphill.

It wasn't the pills she was addicted to. It was the grief, the simultaneous struggle to clutch her pain to her chest as she once had my brother and to push it as far away as possible, as though by gaining distance from his loss she could make it less real.

She'd been up early again this morning, softly clanging about the kitchen, but I stayed in my room until I heard her climb the stairs and shut her door. My dad's words nested themselves in my ears. *"Don't provoke her, Olivia. She's hurting."*

Weren't we all?

Kara was at the door two minutes to twelve. I opened it and stepped outside, the taste of regret in my mouth.

She looked me over. "Hold still." She reached into a pocket of the impossibly tight jeans she wore and pulled out a stubby eye pencil with a gold lid. She had me look up while she ran it just under my bottom lashes, following that with a smudge of her thumb.

Her breath smelled like cinnamon.

"Let's go."

I followed her down the street, trying not to notate all the very visible differences between us. Her shirt was short and sheer in the back, exposing a dark lace bra. My V-neck was loose and too big in the shoulders, creating a webbed effect at the armpits. Her hair was seductively rumpled where mine was flat, her figure ample where mine was lean. Her stride bobbed along the surface of some invisible current the rest of us weren't privy to. I towed behind, slipping underwater.

She took liberties.

I was among them.

Prescott was too.

We arrived wordlessly at his door. Kara held back while I knocked. The door opened, and his dimples preceded him by at least two seconds.

"You're not going to believe this, but my dad's battery was dead this morning. He took my car to work." Prescott spoke to me but looked at Kara.

I turned to her, waiting.

"Olivia can drive."

I couldn't argue. Hadn't I known somehow this was

coming? Hadn't I expected as much when I deferred to her for a solution? I sighed, the weight of Prescott's eyes and dimples pressing down on me. "Let me get the keys."

They walked behind me back down to my house. Their chatter was light as birds in the morning. I could picture the easy smiles, the sideways glances. I didn't need eyes in the back of my head. I was an unnecessary chaperone.

I left them at the open front door as I went inside and climbed the stairs. My mother's room was near dark, and she was out cold. She would wake while I was gone, go to the bathroom, maybe watch some television. And she would never notice my absence.

I shuffled through the items on her dresser until my fingers felt the cold resistance of metal teeth. I swiped them up, and the keys came together loudly in my hand. I glanced at the bed. No movement. I turned to go and found Kara standing silently in the doorway.

Her eyes went from me, to my mother, to me again. I froze as she stepped into the room, looking at shapes in the dimness. She picked up several pill bottles, reading the labels, setting them down again. I swallowed. There were a variety of antidepressants and anxiety meds: Xanax, Ativan, Valium, Klonopin, Wellbutrin, Prozac, Effexor. Then there were the painkillers: OxyContin, Percodan. *Depression hurts*, the ads would read. Opiates prescribed for a broken heart. Then there were the sleep aids: Ambien, Lunesta, Halcion. The doctors couldn't resist a mother with a dead child. They gave her anything she wanted. And over the last three years, she'd tried nearly everything on the market at least once.

Kara emptied half a dozen Ativan into the palm of her hand and grinned at me. "For later," she whispered.

I wanted to stop her, but the surrealism of seeing another person here, in this space, of having this shame unwrapped like a gift by a total stranger, rendered me powerless. I just watched her as if I were watching a made-for-TV drama. She moved across to the dresser and picked up a small jewelry box. After bringing it over, she set it on the bed for better light and opened it right next to where my mother was sleeping. The chipped wood lid had been inlaid with an art deco, mother-of-pearl design. It managed a small glint even in the shadows of the folds of the comforter.

Kara pushed a finger around inside and pulled out a white gold and aquamarine ring that had been my grandmother's before it became my mother's. She slipped it on her middle finger and held it up, appraising. She looked up at me from where she knelt on the floor. She asked no questions, made no excuses. She simply dared me to do or say anything.

I didn't.

Rising, she slipped the lid back on the box and shoved it onto the nightstand crowded with bottles and old glasses of water. "Come on. Let's get out of here."

I followed her out of my mother's room, my grandmother's ring on her swinging right hand. When we got downstairs, Prescott was standing in the kitchen near the wall. He ran a finger over an indent in the Sheetrock at eye level, handing a large shard of glass out on his other palm toward me. "This was embedded in your wall."

I took it and dropped it in the trash. Kara's eyes rested on me with the burden of calculation. I looked at Prescott. "I broke a glass the other night."

"Something would have had to have exploded to get all the way up there."

Something did, but it wasn't the glass.

I ignored him and held up the keys. "Come on. I'll drive."

I'd never cared about the ring. But now my eyes kept sliding sideways to where it circled Kara's finger. It looked kind of ridiculous next to the chipped black polish on her nails. I should have said something. I still could. A piece of me wanted desperately to protect my mother, defend her while she was vulnerable. But the larger part of me felt her hands ripping out my hair and saw the glass lying in Prescott's palm. What was there to defend anymore? Maybe I liked seeing someone take advantage of her. It meant they acknowledged the hopelessness of the situation. The absurdity of the day was summarized in that ring.

My mother's car was immaculate inside. It smelled like leather seats and plastic. Her Unity Realty For Sale signs were still in the trunk. I could hear them sliding against one another when we turned a corner.

Kara had the stereo on and was resetting all the stations. Prescott was in the back seat, his good looks filling up the rearview mirror.

I was behind the wheel, choking on my unease.

"So where are we going?" Kara asked, angling so she could look at both Prescott and me.

My eyes found Prescott's in the rearview. I hadn't planned

this, so I didn't know where to take Kara. I was heading in the general direction of the mall.

"Let's eat. I'm starving," he supplied. He suggested a hole-in-the-wall pizza place off West Little York.

I shrugged and complied.

I didn't eat. It was impossible when crammed in a tiny booth, cornered between Prescott's dimples and golden biceps, Kara's cinnamon lip gloss, and my grandmother's stolen ring. The aquamarine kept winking at me from her finger, a cold, accusing eye in its band of icy gold. It was the color of the Aegean Sea as I would have imagined it. That color belonged in Kara's world, not mine.

"What kind of name is Prescott anyway?" Kara asked as she placed a pepperoni on her tongue.

I didn't imagine anyone had ever dared to ask such a question of him before. I watched him from over the bubbles of my fountain drink, watched the way his eyelids dipped and his biceps tightened. Watched one corner of his mouth rise in a pleased way. Watched his weight shift on his elbows. He was a penny she set spinning on the table. He was circling for a place to land.

"A Republican one," he said finally with a laugh.

Kara made a pout. "Are you as stuffy as it makes you sound?"

He looked at Kara. He looked at me. "I don't know. Ask Olivia. She's known me a long time."

Kara cut her blue-gray eyes in my direction. This was a game for her, putting us all on the cusp of some social precipice, watching us dangle.

I tensed. Bit my straw. Released. "He's all right."

Prescott burst out laughing. "Thanks for the winning endorsement."

Kara grinned proudly at me. I'd told a joke I wasn't in on. But I half smiled back, feigning intention.

I caught him looking at me four times after that.

Lunch was followed by the mall. I had no money for either. Mostly I followed Kara around. Watched her shoplift a set of bracelets and a hair band. Talked to Prescott while she tried on clothes she had no intention of buying.

I'd meant what I said at lunch. Prescott wasn't like other guys with marble statue faces. He played basketball but wasn't a total jock. He read books. He didn't cheat in class or sleep around. He wasn't a complete asshole. You couldn't hate him for winning the genetic lottery, even if you wanted to. But he was still unreachable in so many ways. It's not like he wasn't aware of how he looked. It showed in the way he carried himself. The confidence born to those who haven't suffered, who know they'll never have to.

Kara, though, wasn't like anyone else. She wasn't a cheerleader or a beauty pageant wannabe. She didn't act like the popular girls in my, or any other, grade. She didn't look like them either, though she could have. It was more like she didn't care to, didn't have to. And she was all the more irresistible for it. She had one of the hottest guys in school sitting outside her dressing room after meeting her once. She stole things she probably could have bought just as easily. She poured magnetism into every gesture without breaking a sweat. She was the epitome of effortless. But not grace. There was nothing graceful about her. She was raw. She was salt in the wound.

She could cure. She could kill.

The mall got old fast. We piled back into my mother's car and rolled the windows down. It was late afternoon. The car was so hot the seat belt buckles could leave third-degree burns.

"I want to go swimming," Kara moaned from the passenger's seat.

"I know an apartment complex they're going to tear down," Prescott replied. "They haven't drained the pool yet." Prescott's dad was a contractor.

Kara beamed.

"We don't have suits," I said to no one in particular. I hated pools.

"That's what makes it interesting," Kara responded, arching her brows.

Inside me, the panic balled itself up like a fist around my heart, squeezing mercilessly. Pools were now a Foster family taboo. We didn't keep them, we didn't talk about them, and we certainly didn't swim in them. We tried, as much as possible, to not even see them. If you didn't look at them directly, you could almost pretend they weren't there, tell yourself it was just a large puddle or painted concrete and not the silent killer you knew it to be, an open maw waiting patiently to swallow families whole.

But I didn't want to show weakness. I wanted Kara and Prescott to see me as more than a three-year-old accident. Maybe if they did, I could too. My eyes met Prescott's in the rearview again. "Lead the way."

We stopped at a corner store for Kara to grab a drink. She came out sporting a twenty-ounce Coke, a bottle of cheap red gas station wine, and three plastic cups.

"How'd you get that?" Prescott asked as she climbed back in, obviously impressed.

"I have my methods."

The apartment pool had an iron fence, but the gate wasn't locked. All the rows had been evacuated, and several windowpanes were busted out where squatters had gotten in. There was no lounge furniture or umbrellas, but there were a few scattered chairs, water, and a running filter still—probably an oversight.

Kara passed me the wine bottle once we were inside. "Open this."

It was a screw top. I gave it a twist and held it out to her.

She poured equal parts wine and Coke into a cup. "Everyone drinks this in Spain," she said, handing it to me. "Take a sip."

I shrugged and did as commanded, wondering how she knew what people in Spain were drinking. It wasn't like I'd never tasted wine before. My mom used to let me have a small glass every New Year's Eve since I turned ten. This was a bitter comparison though. It was thin and sour and burned the back of my throat. I was grateful for the Coke.

I passed my cup to Prescott as Kara fiddled in her pocket.

"Aha!" she cried. She shoved a fist between us and unrolled her fingers. The six Ativan rested innocuously in her sticky palm.

Prescott winced from the drink and looked from me to her. "What's that?"

"A good time," Kara said, pleased with herself. "It's Ativan. Just takes the edge off. Courtesy of Olivia's mom."

Prescott looked at me, and I looked away. I knew people knew. How could they not know? But feeling their knowing was different than seeing it in front of you. His pity thickened the air like soup. Pity was always worse than ignorance.

"Just take it," I said to shift the energy. I snatched a couple of little white pentagons from Kara's palm and popped them in my mouth, seizing the cup out of Prescott's hand to wash them down with. My eyes moved to the still surface of the water in the pool before me as I passed the bottle back. I was dimly aware of Prescott and Kara swallowing the pills. But mostly I was staring at the water thinking that I would need the medication to do this—to sit here and not remember.

It was the splash that broke my stupor.

Kara was in the water, her jeans and shirt abandoned in a heap at our feet. For a while, we just watched her gliding from one end of the pool to the next, holding her breath long enough to be half-porpoise.

Maybe it was just the drugs, but it felt like she was under for ten minutes before Prescott said, "What do you think of our new neighbor?"

I could feel my body letting down from the medication. A warm, soft wave crested inside me, broke, spilled over, and crested again.

I realized then she was as unreachable to him as he was to me.

The heat pressed my body into the concrete beneath us. I took another sip of my drink. "I think I like her."

CHAPTER 8

It was weird being with Prescott again. The intimacy of childhood returned, but the wall of adolescence was still there, and I couldn't ignore it. Somehow, only Kara made it work.

When he finally got up the nerve to get in the water, I buried myself in my drink as he undressed next to me. He left his boxers on, but it didn't make the burn of him any less palpable until he was fully immersed.

I worried they'd find each other under the water. That I'd be sitting like some kind of voyeur on the sidelines. But Kara circled him, kept her distance. If a move was to be made, it was hers to make it. And despite the fact that she'd already stolen from me, I understood that that wasn't what this was about. Though it brought me no nearer to her true motives.

She liked his eyes on her.

She liked mine on her too.

Beyond that, who could say?

"Olivia! Come in!" She bobbed up onto the pavement and

stood dripping before me.

"I'm good."

"Don't be silly. We're not going to let you just sit here while we have all the fun." She grabbed my arm and tugged on it.

I pulled back. "Really. I'm fine. Go on."

She pulled harder, yanking me from my chair.

"Kara, I don't swim!"

She laughed. "If you can drive, you can swim."

Prescott looked tense behind her.

"I didn't say I can't swim. I said I *don't*." I jerked my arm back again.

Kara's smile faltered. She looked back at Prescott. He shrugged with a guilty expression.

She stepped close to me, close enough that the water dripping off her spotted my shirt and wetted the tops of my feet. She placed a hand against my neck, moving her lips close to my ear. "You'll be with me," she whispered. "I promise it'll be okay."

Cinnamon. Heat. The delicious wave of Ativan rising within me. Her thumb tracing little circles against my skin. I nodded, unable to speak.

"Take those off," she said, pointing at my jeans and stepping back.

"I keep the shirt." There was no way I was stripping down in front of them.

Kara nodded. "Whatever you say, Olives."

When I took my jeans off, she led me to the water's edge. I lowered myself into the pool, my hand in Kara's the whole time.

I hadn't even taken a bath since Robby died.

Underwater, time stood still. I sunk beneath the surface, holding my eyes open and my breath against the tides stirring both within me and without. I watched Kara's and Prescott's legs ripple and glow and move in slow motion. His were always inching toward. Hers were always dancing away.

I wondered if this was how Robby felt in his last moments—suspended. The whole world on pause.

And then the invisible knife of breath began to shred my lungs. The chlorine filled my eyes with liquid fire. And the weightlessness I first experienced grew heavy with panic.

I, too, was drowning.

I fought my own inclination to rise.

I tensed up, curling into a ball, refusing to surface. I pushed back from within. Holding…holding. I could do this. I could see what he saw, feel what he felt. I could let go. Disappear. Forget. Implode. I could tear an Olivia-shaped hole through the world. I could wait for the shadow to find me, roll over my skin through the water like a shroud, and release me.

Only, I couldn't.

Just as my own instincts to live overwhelmed me, I felt strong hands clutch at my arms and the drag of twenty thousand gallons of water slide over my skin as the pool was forced to release its grip.

I came up coughing.

"Jesus! Are you trying to drown yourself?" Prescott's voice was shrill compared to Kara's cool tone.

"Olivia," she said as though she were speaking to a naughty child. "Olivia, just breathe."

I wretched over the side of the pool, red wine and Coke

splashing across the concrete like a warning.

I gasped and the air came, and it was a thousand times more painful than the want of it. Living shattered me.

Kara ran her hand over my wet hair, tucking it away from my face, rubbing my shoulders. "Breathe, Olives. You're okay."

Prescott hovered behind us, the water bobbing at the level of his naked chest. "Should we go?"

Kara spun. "No. Just give her a minute."

I backed away from the concrete ledge, splashing pool water across my face and over my hair. I cleared my eyes and stared hard at the boy who always seemed to be around to witness when my life was going to pieces. "I'm fine. We stay."

We stayed until the sun melted beyond the vacant apartment buildings and the first sad show of suburban stars splattered across a charcoal smudge of a sky. We stayed until the booze was all gone and our skin wrinkled across the pads of our fingers like dried figs. We stayed until the little, five-sided pills lost their sweet grasp on our systems, the rise and fall of the drug ebbing into a soft, steady hum. We stayed until the world settled into its rightful place around us.

Kara was the first out of the pool. "Let's go," she said casually as Prescott and I continued laughing at a joke only the three of us could understand. "I'm bored."

My laughter faded as I looked up, noticing the evening's descent for the first time. I scrambled to the pool's edge, dragging myself from the water. "Oh shit! What time is it?"

Prescott followed me out. "I dunno. Can't be past nine," he said, guessing.

Kara buttoned her shorts and glanced at the cell phone stuffed in her pocket. "It's eight thirty, Olives. Why?"

"Fuck," I spat. "My dad is going to kill me."

I had taken the car. The thought was still swimming in the miasma of my mind. *I took the car.*

"Do you have a curfew?" Prescott looked confused.

Even confusion looked gorgeous on him, I noticed with a frown. "No." Did I? I wasn't sure. It had never been an issue before. But I was pretty sure I wasn't allowed to take Mom's car without permission and disappear until after dark without a word.

"Don't forget the wine on your breath," Kara said with an impish grin.

And that. I was pretty sure that was not allowed either. Never mind the stolen Ativan. At least that bit would go unnoticed.

And unlike Kara and Prescott, I'd kept my clothes on when I went into the pool. I was sopping wet. Kara had a bloom of wet fabric around each of her breasts, but otherwise, she was dry. Prescott simply turned away, dropped his soggy boxers, and pulled his shorts on.

Kara nodded toward his ass and wiggled her eyebrows at me. Despite my growing fear, I had to stifle a giggle.

I couldn't remember the last time I almost *giggled.*

I found a crusty old towel in Mom's trunk and spread it across the driver's seat. We piled into the car, and I sped for home, dropping Prescott off at his mailbox.

"Until next time, ladies," he said with a salute, a wad of wet boxers in one hand. His grin was brighter than the streetlamp we sat idling under.

I rolled down the road as stealthily as possible, watching the dull white paint of my house inch nearer, the black shutters scowling like furrowed brows. I hit the button to raise the garage door and winced when it rumbled loudly. I pulled in and turned off the engine. My dad was bound to come storming out at any moment. My eyes fixed on the interior door.

"Relax, Olives," Kara said breathily as she opened the back door and climbed out. She came around to my side and opened my door for me. "What's he gonna do? Ground you? You spend all your time inside anyway."

I stood and closed the door quietly behind me. "How do you know? You just moved here."

Kara's eyes lighted on mine like dancing sparrows and her face broke into a wide, sun-filled smile. "Don't sass me, Olives." She was teasing me. "Or I'll keep Prescott all to myself."

She was perfectly capable of it. But I couldn't tell if I was more distraught at the idea of losing him or losing her.

She lifted her hands and began to wiggle the white gold and aquamarine ring off her finger.

I stopped her. "Keep it." She'd earned it.

She dropped her hands, gave me a half smile, leaned in, and kissed me soft and full on the lips, but only for a second. I watched her strut out of my garage and across the street, where the glowing cherry of her grandmother's cigar was waiting in the recesses of the front porch.

My fingers went to my mouth. My lips felt warm and buzzed with a new rush of energy. It had been a friendly kiss…right? Once upon a time, I had been saving those lips for Prescott. Not when we were young and sticky with sweat and chewing gum and innocence, but later, when our bodies started changing and his smile broadened and his dimples deepened along with his voice.

I always believed Prescott would be my first kiss. I'm not sure when I really stopped believing it, or that I ever did. It just ceased to matter after Robby died, like a lot of things—celebrity crushes, school gossip, trending haircuts, what brand of jeans were in or out. I guess I was still saving my lips for someone.

But now, I flushed, thinking that might have just changed—that Kara Hallas with her too-tight clothes and her messy hair and her inborn irreverence might have become my first kiss. I swallowed the lump in my throat and hit the button to lower the garage door. Turning to the interior door, I placed a shaky hand on the knob.

Steel yourself, Olives, I thought with sudden panic. However angry my dad was, it could never be as bad as when my mother lost it. I'd been through much worse already.

My heart thudded a drumbeat in my chest as the door swung open. The kitchen was dark, the lights all out. Had he gone to bed already?

I stepped inside, tensing for the confrontation. And then the clouds of my mind parted, and a gloomy realization dawned with a half-spent sun. He wasn't home. His car wasn't in the garage or the driveway. I'd been too spaced out on booze and pills and Kara to notice.

My shoulders slid down, and my heart sunk with them. It was only then I understood how disappointed I was. I'd *wanted* to get in trouble. Wanted to hear him shout and make demands and punish me. I'd wanted to *exist*. Like I did in the pool. But the gravity of my afternoon adventure dissipated into ether as I crossed the threshold.

I closed the door and flipped on the light.

My mother sat silently at the table.

For a split second, the rush of fear came back to me—of hope. But she didn't even look up.

"Where's Dad?" I asked her.

She rocked back and forth in her chair, her eyes downcast.

That's when I noticed it, the wide, blue-checked book in front of her with the tattered corners. It was a photo album. Robby's photo album. I didn't know it was still in the house.

I moved to the table and stood across from her, looking down on the vinyl cover with the yellow duck.

She didn't have the courage to open it.

I wanted to turn the pages, to see his feathery hair and crooked smile. To see the baby fat as it collected around his wrists and remember the heat and smell of him. But I didn't have the courage to open it either.

I moved toward the stairs, turned back, and looked at her once more. "He's dead, Mom," I said quietly, no longer caring if I set her off or not.

Silent tears slipped down her cheeks as she rocked, but still, she didn't see me.

I turned the light out on her and climbed the stairs. *He's dead*, I thought again. *We all are.*

How silly of me to forget.

CHAPTER 9

In my dream that night, the pool was just as it had been with Kara and Prescott. My body hummed inside, my skin slick as a seal's pelt as I sank beneath the surface of the water. My eyes stung with the chlorine, but I forced them open as I watched Prescott's legs waver like a mirage in the distance.

I moved toward them, only vaguely aware that the bottom was sloping away beneath me. The water grew dark and soft in the deep end, and I lost sight of Prescott, myself, anyone.

And then hands plunged in from above, pressing down on me with a giant's strength. At first, I thought it was Prescott. He was drowning me. I opened my mouth to scream but only bubbles emerged. They floated up to an invisible surface where they broke without a sound. I struggled and thrashed against them and became aware that they weren't Prescott's hands at all, but Kara's.

Long, slender fingers tangled in my hair. My grandmother's aquamarine ring glinted in the water like lost treasure. I fought her, but she was so strong, so unbelievably strong. My lungs were folding. Panic consumed me. And as I wrapped my hands around her wrists to try and free myself, I realized it had never been Kara at all, but my own mother. As the last breath left me, I looked up and saw her face like a broken reflection through the water. She was smiling. I couldn't remember the last time I'd seen her smile.

I sunk like silt to the floor, and Robby was next to me. His blue eyes were fixed open and staring. His yellow hair wafted around his face. His skin was the color of ashes.

I woke up trembling. My sheets were wrapped around me half a dozen times from all the thrashing. And my bed was soaked.

I hadn't wet the bed since I was four.

Dad was in the laundry room when I carried my sheets down to wash. He was ironing his tie for work.

"Hey, kiddo," he said with a smile that never reached his eyes.

"Hey." My voice was flat as day-old soda.

"Rough night?" he asked, eyeing the wad of cotton in my arms.

I opened the wash and shoved the sheets in, dumping a scoop of white-blue powder detergent over them. "Bad dream."

He picked his tie up and began fastening it under his collar. "Well, I'm late. Keep an eye on your mother for me. See you tonight."

His cologne lingered in the little room long after he left.

We'd been out there since about ten o'clock that morning.

I'd pretended to check the mailbox but really was checking

to see if anyone was outside when she called me over. I'd spent three days in my room after our unsanctioned excursion with Prescott, trying to go back to life before Kara. But I'd had a taste of something more than cheap wine that day, and it awoke a hunger in me that wouldn't subside.

Kara was sprawled across her front lawn, her eyes hidden behind an oversize pair of black sunglasses circa 1984. Her hair streamed like honey between the blades of grass. Her knees were up and her feet were bare. Her toenails had been re-painted poison apple green.

"I'm so bored," she moaned under the sun. "I mean, could it get any *hotter*?"

I was folded over myself on the steps of her front porch. "They say it's the hottest season on record, with the drought."

"I believe them."

"We could go inside," I suggested.

"Your house?" She shot up and tugged her sunglasses down, fixing her steel-and-denim eyes on me.

"No. I meant yours."

Kara frowned. "It's just as boring in there. And the whole place reeks of Sybil's cigars."

She said this last bit in an especially loud voice aimed at the screen door, as though hoping her grandmother would hear.

I shrugged. "Can't be worse than being out here in the heat."

Kara stood and stretched, scratching the back of a thigh. "Fine. Let's go in." She breezed past me toward the door, and I quickly scrambled up to follow.

We passed a formal living room. It was small and had

fading floral wallpaper across the top half of the walls. The bottom was covered in dark wood wainscoting. There was an overstuffed armchair in shorn red velveteen and an old record player on turned legs. A Victorian lamp that looked like a French coachman from Versailles holding a lantern glowed in one corner while a statue of a veiled woman, maybe three or four feet tall, stood with a vase of dried wheat before her in another.

Sybil sat in her rocker beside a smoking table, puffing away at a fat stub of cigar. Her milky eyes skimmed over us, unseeing.

Kara waved a hand in front of her face and made a retching noise. "Did you hear me out there, Yaya? I said *it stinks.*"

The old woman grunted. "You talk too much," she retorted.

Kara rolled her eyes at me. She danced up to the record player and began to flip through an assortment of old vinyl that was stored beneath.

I stood in the doorway, feeling Sybil somehow study me with preternatural eyes.

Kara placed a record delicately on the turntable, setting the needle in position. A scratchy tune replete with violins and chimes began to pour out, and a woman's high and tremulous voice echoed above them in a French melody.

"Josephine Baker," Kara informed me before reaching down for her Yaya's cigar. Quick as a snake, she snatched it from Sybil's mouth, placed it between her own lips, and took a long drag as she twirled around the room to the haunting tones of the record.

Sybil's fingers tightened on the arm of her chair, and her face twisted into a look of frustration, but Kara only laughed, smoke billowing out as she did, and thrust the cigar back at her.

As Sybil recovered it with one hand, she grabbed hold of Kara's wrist with the other, her grip tightening like raptor talons as she pulled Kara's hand before her face.

"What are you doing?" Kara whined, but she was unable to pull away.

In the light slipping through the blinds, my grandmother's aquamarine ring glinted on Kara's captured hand.

"What's this?" she hissed, her dead gaze fixed on the ring.

Kara squirmed. The record began to skip, and Josephine Baker's shrill soprano rang the same note over and over again.

"Olivia gave it to me," she said, finally breaking free of the old woman's grasp. She quickly moved to the record player to lift the needle.

Sybil leaned back in her chair, her face void of expression. "You?" she asked after a moment. "You think you're hiding there? Think I can't see you?"

I didn't know what to say, so I kept silent, edging deeper into the room.

Sybil smiled. "I may be the *only* one who sees you, girl."

Kara placed the record back in its sleeve. "Yaya, stop it," she said, joining me at my side. "You'll scare her."

"Good," the old woman huffed. "That's why we came."

Kara rolled her eyes again and twirled a finger by her ear, making the international sign for crazy.

I stepped toward the statue in the corner, feigning interest as an excuse to get away from Sybil. "Catholic?" I asked, pointing at what I assumed was Mary. I didn't know many other veiled women who got enshrined in statuary.

"Hardly," Kara snorted.

I gave her a perplexed look.

She grabbed my arm, pulling me closer to the gray, waist-high figure. "*This* is Demeter Chthonia," she chirped as though introducing me to a favorite pet.

I raised one eyebrow at her in confusion.

"You know. From the myths—the ones with dark chariots and abducted girls."

I shook my head, vaguely recalling a story in my literature class two years back about a maiden who was kidnapped by the king of Hell and whose mother refused to make the crops grow until she was returned. Demeter had been the mother's name, but she seemed a world away from the gloomy figure draped before me.

"She's the Mother of the Dead," Kara supplied, growing strangely serious for a moment. "She's very old. The statue, I mean. She's been in our family for a long time."

I stared into the near-featureless face, every stone fold falling convincingly over the head and shoulders with the lightness of a silk wrap.

"Yaya collects things," Kara added, gesturing with her eyes around the room at the lamp, the record player, and other artifacts of their family. "*Old* things. Demeter and Yaya keep each other company," Kara whispered as an aside.

At that, Sybil sniffed. "Ridiculous child," she muttered. "We collect the dead," she said, stiffening.

Kara snickered and pulled me away toward the stairs, away from her family heirlooms and her grandmother. "She's totally losing it," she whispered as we ascended. "Blind *and* senile, poor thing."

But somehow I didn't believe either was true.

Kara's room was small and square like any other, and yet it felt like I'd been granted admission into some secret place, a speakeasy or boudoir belonging to a famous courtesan, the hideout of vigilante gangsters. Across the hall, the master bedroom's door loomed large and breathless, closed over the final moments of its former occupant.

Kara closed her door, cutting off my focus. I blinked a few times and looked at her. She stood expressionless before me. "The beams still creak at night," she said pointedly.

I looked at her door again, to where I knew the master bedroom lay beyond. "Do you believe in ghosts?" I asked.

Kara shrugged and flopped on her bed. "I believe in everything."

I sat down next to her.

"Do you?" she asked.

We were a family of ghosts, how could I not? "Yeah, I guess."

She nodded once and stretched for a spiral notebook sitting atop some papers on her nightstand. Her shirt pulled up over her navel as she did, exposing the puckered dip in her flesh.

I looked away.

It was then I began to really take in my surroundings. Spare furniture, no wall hangings to speak of. A couple of empty boxes stacked in one corner and an open closet door revealing an explosion of clothes. There was an old-fashioned vanity by the bed with a large silvered mirror that had gone dull in spots. A black bistro chair sat before it, the canes that formed the back looping into a curly heart shape over the seat.

Kara held a sparkly pink pen in one hand with a giant rainbow eraser on top. She had the eraser poised between her teeth like she was thinking.

"Why have an eraser on a pen?" I asked her, then kicked myself for the awkwardness of the question.

She rested her eyes on me, then held the eraser before her face, studying it. "Dunno," she said with a pouted bottom lip. "I just like it."

Her spiral had a worn lavender cover with a glitter-covered skull and crossbones sticker in the bottom left-hand corner. The remnants of a dozen torn-out pages were trying to escape their wiry, spiraled bonds. "What's in the notebook?"

Kara looked from it to me. "I write to my pen pals in this notebook," she said. "Then I tear the letters out and mail them in decorated envelopes."

She wasn't the sort I took for having pen pals. But the Hallases obviously had foreign roots. Maybe she had distant cousins or something. "What kind of pen pals?"

Kara's lips twisted slowly into a wicked grin. She tossed her pen on the bed and reached for a stack of papers on her nightstand, passing them to me.

I looked down at the first. A staple in the top left-hand corner held the envelope to the back of it. It was a piece of ordinary notebook paper. The ink was blue and the script slanted far to the left, with sharp, narrow loops on certain letters. I looked up at Kara, a question poised on my face.

"Go ahead." She shrugged, beaming. "Read them."

I began hesitantly with the first.

Darling Kara,

How are you? Your last letter was a ray of sunshine in this dark place. Thank you for the picture. It was good to put a face to the voice in your letters. You are more beautiful than I even dreamed. I keep it pinned on the corkboard right next to my bed.

Thank you for believing me—

The words *believing me* had been crossed out and replaced.

—believing in me. In my innocence. The world is a cruel place, and this place is crueler still.

I have a job now. I clean the prison gym twice a week.

My eyes shot up to Kara's, but she didn't seem to notice the shock lacing my gaze. I looked back to the letter.

It's menial work but it's something. It pays very little. Enough to buy this paper and a couple pens once a month. As to your question, you cannot send me anything besides your letters and the enclosed picture. Thank you for trying to include the blank paper, but they only took it away.

You have the most beautiful smile.

I never touched that woman. I found her that way was all. You know that. I know that. Someday the world will know it.

There was more, but I couldn't stomach reading it. I flipped the paper over and looked at the envelope. The return address read *John Willhelm, Florida State Prison, Box 979, Raiford, FL, 32026.*

My eyes caught the handwriting on the next page, dated June 5 in loose, loopy writing that looked practically scribbled onto the page.

Dear Kara Hallas, it began.

I was so happy to receive your letter. How old are you? May I ask? I receive letters from all over the country. Everyone is interested in death row except those of us who live here.

It went on to talk about the weather, the results of his latest appeal, and what he had for dinner the night before. There was a doodle on the second page of a large, black spider wearing a bow tie. The ink was smeared on his signature, but I could make out the name—

Craig West.

I remembered him from the news. He'd been convicted of killing seven women in Texas and New Mexico only two years before. His envelope was torn and taped over with a Band-Aid in one corner.

I flipped through the rest. They were all the same. All men. All prisoners. Murderers, rapists, who knew what else? Some were perfectly congenial, as though she'd been writing to members of the teachers' union or soldiers at an out-of-state base. Others were riddled with expletives, even graphic accounts of how they'd "make her squeal" or "pleasure" her if they met. Some professed love. Others just seemed grateful for the mere acknowledgment. But all—*all*—were criminals.

I finally dropped the papers in my lap and looked at her, my mouth hollow and open as a flytrap.

Kara grinned. "Cool, right?"

"Cool?" My tone was severe. "Kara, these men are convicts!"

Her face contorted defensively. "I know. Duh. You think I addressed the prison by accident?"

"I think maybe you're taking more than my mother's pills. You don't believe all this babble about innocence, do you?"

Kara snatched the letters from my lap. "Course not. I choose my pen pals carefully. I research them before I write."

"And you're sending them pictures? Are you mad?" I wasn't sure what to do here. Was there someone I reported this to? A school counselor? A cop?

"Relax, Olives," Kara droned, depositing her letters back on her nightstand. "These guys are lifers. Half of them are on death row. They're not going anywhere, least of all coming after me."

I felt a little stupid but no less baffled. "Why do you do it?"

She drifted to her vanity and picked up a tube of lip gloss, swiping her lips with a bashful pink glaze. "Why not? This stuff's worth money, you know. Ever heard of murderabilia? People are auctioning off crap like this online for hundreds, even thousands. These guys are gold mines."

She reached into her closet and emerged with a stack of shoeboxes. They all held letters, pictures, drawings. One had a tiny origami bug made of gum wrappers. Another had a carefully drawn map showing important places in a crime scene.

Kara picked up a small self-portrait drawn in markers on a torn piece of yellow legal paper. It had a scrawled signature in one corner. "This right here is worth over seven hundred dollars easy."

My fingers brushed against a lock of hair in one of the boxes and I cringed. "This is sick."

Her face grew sullen. "They're still human beings," she added, jumping up to snatch the boxes back from me.

She tucked them carefully back into the recesses of her closet as tenderly as a mother tucking her child in for a nap. Then she turned to me. "Do you work, Olivia?"

I was baffled by her sudden change of topic. "What?"

"Do you w-o-r-k? Like a job? You know, for money?" She said this last bit while rubbing her thumb and fingertips together.

I shook my head. "No. I told you, I don't have a car."

"Right. And how do you think you're going to get one, sitting around that dungeon you call a house all day? It's a catch-22, isn't it? Can't work without a car but can't buy a car without a job."

"I don't know. I hadn't really thought about it." I was embarrassed all of a sudden, keenly aware that this was supposed to matter to me. People my age are supposed to think of little else besides cars and freedom—and sex, of course. But those things rarely, if ever, crossed my mind.

"You think I really want to spend the rest of my life traipsing around behind a trail of Yaya's cigar smoke? Huh? You think I want to be trapped with my mom and my grandmother the rest of my days?"

"No, I—"

"Of course I don't. But I guess you didn't think about that because you have Daddy to give you money when you need it, to buy you stuff and send you to college. In case you didn't notice, Olivia, I don't have that."

I wasn't sure what to say. Our neighborhood wasn't featured on HGTV, but people were hardly hurting for cash around here. Even if her mother had moved her into the grim foreclosure no else wanted, they obviously had *some* means. But then, what did I know? Kara was right; I spent my days in a fog-filled dungeon of a life, peering out at the world as it passed us by. I had no more ambitions, no goals, no direction. I'd lost touch with what it felt like to *crave* something.

"One box of this stuff sold to the right bidder could easily buy me a decent car. All of them combined might pay my college tuition, or at least part of it. How else do you think I pay for my clothes, my things?"

I hadn't thought about it. Why would I? I just assumed her parents paid like everyone else's around here. I felt foolish. "I don't know. I'm sorry."

She softened a little at the edges, like petals beginning to curl, and sunk into her vanity chair. "I know it's…*different*."

My eyebrows shot up.

"Okay," she conceded. "It's weird. I know that. But we don't get to choose our families or the circumstances we're born into. This, this gives me a way out, a way to something more."

"So why keep it in your closet? All this…what did you call it? *Murderabilia?* Why not sell it if you need money?"

She huffed. "It's not that simple, Olives. I do sell it, but you can't just throw this shit on eBay, you know. I have to list it through a site on the dark web. It takes time—time to get the right pictures, to upload the content, to wait for the right buyer. And some of these items appreciate in value, especially after certain *events*."

I didn't like the way she emphasized that last word. "What events?"

She shrugged. "You know, once their appeals run out. Once other investigations and charges are complete. Once they're executed or the victims or their families die."

I scowled.

"I know, I know," she said, brushing me off. "It's dark. I get it. But I don't make the rules. It just works that way. Some things I keep to allow their value to increase while I'm selling other things. It's just how the game is played."

I took a heavy breath. "And you don't think it's dangerous?"

She grinned, brimming with mischief. "What's life without a little danger?"

When I didn't smile back, she added, "Regardless of what everyone thinks, they're just people like you and me."

More like monsters, but I didn't say it. And most people weren't like me, or Kara, for that matter. "Do your mom and grandmother know?"

She spun around in her chair and sprayed a cloud of Miss Dior perfume at my face. "What difference does it make?"

I didn't know how to answer that.

CHAPTER 10

Kara was hungry. She was busy repainting her nails and so couldn't be expected to lift a thing. She sent me downstairs to forage for drinks and snacks of some kind and return with what pickings I could find.

I made my way down the flight of stairs cautiously, my eyes glued to the closed master bedroom until it was no longer in view. I'm not sure what I expected. It wasn't likely Mr. Dearing was going to swing it wide and say, "Boo!" And in truth, the house felt less his with Kara here. Had it only been blind, old Sybil and bustling Rhea, his presence might have been stronger, still holding the second story captive as he had since the day he'd tied his noose. But Kara was all life and reckless audacity. Her spirit chased the others away.

Downstairs, I found the kitchen and spun into it quickly, avoiding the front of the house and Sybil.

The kitchen was as I remembered it—white, open, airy, and well lit. The countertops were made of light stone, and pale wooden stools lined the bar. A large, double-door fridge sat in the center of a wall of white-painted cabinets. I pulled it open and rooted around, dragging out two root beers and a tub of ranch dip. When I let the doors swing closed, Rhea was standing behind them, grinning at me.

"Oh," I exclaimed, nearly dropping one of the cans.

She reached for it before I could. "Did I frighten you?"

I gave a tight smile. "Startled is all."

Kara's mom had the same lusty verve her daughter wore like a well-tended finish. But the patina of age had dulled her gleam some, and her soft and round places had grown softer and rounder with years. Still, I could see the likeness of her in Kara and imagine how she must have shone in her youth. I doubted she had any trouble capturing the interest of men even now. I wondered what Kara's father had been like.

"Hungry?" Rhea opened the pantry and sifted through bags and boxes on a shelf, passing me an unopened bag of potato chips and a tray of half-eaten cookies. "These are Kara's favorite," she said, pointing to the cookies.

I piled my finds on the countertop.

"Let me get you something to carry all this up in," Rhea said, turning to another cabinet full of serving trays and folded grocery bags.

Rhea was so nice, getting a tray—it was a very *mom* thing to do. My heart seized remembering a time when doing *mom* things was something my own mom was good at. A little bubble of envy floated up my throat, but I swallowed it down, thinking of Kara's rant about not having her dad around. I couldn't imagine Rhea being okay with the letters Kara had shown me—her *hobby* for money. But surely Rhea had seen the envelopes in the mailbox as they arrived? I had to be certain for my own peace.

"Do you know about Kara's pen pals?" I blurted. Grace had never been my gift.

Rhea spun toward me, a deep plastic tray in her hands. Her smile faltered. "It would be hard to miss the envelopes," she said with a forced laugh. "They come every week."

She set the tray down and began loading our snacks onto it.

"And you're fine with it?" My throat felt thick as felted wool.

Her eyes were cast down, but her smile faded completely.

"You don't think it's wrong or...or dangerous?"

Rhea looked up at me, wearing a mask of resignation. "It's her nature," she said plainly. "And if I have learned anything in my forty-odd years, it is that there is no use fighting nature."

"But—"

Rhea cut me off. "Olivia, you seem like a nice girl. A smart girl. You've only known my Kara a few days, but I think you see more than most. You are...*observant* for someone so young. Tell me, do you find her easy to manage?"

I thought of my grandmother's aquamarine ring winking like the surface of the sea next to Kara's fuchsia nail polish. I found her irresistible. "No."

Rhea nodded and pushed the tray at me. "Kara has always been a willful child. Her interests are unusual, I admit. But she comes by it naturally. Her father..." Rhea sighed. "I see him in her more and more the older she gets."

"What was he like?" The question was out before I could catch it.

Rhea stared at me for a long moment before responding. "He's…*intense.* No one would describe him as a nice man. I can't say I loved him, but I love what he gave me. And we're better off—Kara's better off—without him in our lives. He's where he belongs."

She was gazing out a window as she said this last bit, but then her eyes cut sharply to mine. "Let's hope he stays there."

A chill ran over my skin like a cold breath of air. I'd used the past tense because she'd described him as "gone" before. I couldn't miss that she spoke of him in the present now.

She softened. "Let's just say, there's no changing her. If you haven't learned that by now, you will soon enough."

I felt embarrassed for having brought it up at all. A piece of me wanted to hear more about Kara's father, to understand concretely what Rhea was alluding to. To understand how someone who seemed as kind as she was could be drawn to someone who sounded so sinister and how that explained Kara's strange obsessions, excused them even. But I was already too uncomfortable to stand around waiting for it. I turned with the tray, my face a dozen shades of red, and headed for the doorway.

"She likes you, you know," Rhea called after me. "Kara is very fond of you, Olivia. We all are."

I flashed her a small smile and trotted up the stairs, my gaze now fixed on Kara's door instead of the one across from it.

Once inside, I kicked it closed behind me and laid the tray on Kara's bed. Her fingers were splayed out before her face as she blew on each nail in turn. "Hey." She grinned, pausing to survey the tray's contents. "Good finds."

"Your mom helped me," I admitted.

Kara pointed at a soda can with her chin. "Pop my top?"

My eyes widened as they met hers, and then we both started laughing. I suddenly felt like a child again. A dozen summers flashed before my eyes, summers filled with chlorine and fireworks and sleepovers. Back when my biggest worry would be if my hair would turn green from too much time spent in the pool. When my parents would host barbecues for their work friends and the neighbors, and Prescott and I would play hide-and-seek barefoot along the street. Laughing was something I did before. And root beer. And nail polish. My body remembered them easily, like riding a bike, and gave over to them again as if nothing had changed.

I grinned at Kara and opened her can, passing it to her. While she sipped loudly, I walked around to her nightstand and flipped through the letters once more. Pen pals were a girlish thing, something I could have imagined for myself once. But pen pals who were serial killers were not part of my reverie, no matter how much I wanted to feel normal again.

I rested my hand on top of the stack and heard Rhea's voice speak plainly: *Olivia, you're...a smart girl. You are...observant... She comes by it naturally. Her father... No one would describe him as a "nice man." He's where he belongs.*

And just like that, I understood. Kara's dad must be a convict. If he was in the ranks of these men, then he must be the worst of offenders, a violent felon, a rapist or a killer. My breath caught, and my own family's struggles seemed a million miles away instead of just across the street.

"I have to write a reply to the one on top," she said. "Wanna help me?"

I looked at her, and an invisible hand ran fingers of dread down my spine. I picked up the top letter, the one from John Willhelm. "What'd he do?" I asked, feeling dirty inside for even considering her offer but unable to refuse her.

"You really want to know?"

I nodded, steeling myself.

"He held a woman hostage in her own home for three days. Raped her countless times. Finally squeezed the life out of her and then called the police on himself. Course, once they picked him up, all he could do was sing about his innocence."

The blood drained from my face, and my hands shook ever so slightly. "Just one?"

"One what?" Kara shoved a whole cookie in her mouth, trying not to touch it with her wet nails.

"Victim."

She chewed, swallowed, and guzzled some soda. Her shoulders slid up and down in a characteristic shrug. "They think he might be responsible for a couple of dead prostitutes outside of Miami, but they can't prove it. The police botched the investigations so bad there was no DNA evidence. None that could be trusted, anyway."

My eyebrows went up.

"I told you, I do my research."

I passed the letter to her, and she picked up her spiral notebook and the sparkly pen with the useless eraser. "Dear John," she began out loud.

We wrote three letters in all.

My stomach churned as I helped her think of questions,

carefully choose her phrasing, and research each convict, but I pushed the concerns of my gut away. I was good at that by now, ignoring the pain.

Kara needed this. She needed money, and I wasn't sure what all else, maybe the rush or the danger. But she needed this...*hobby*. And frankly, I needed Kara.

What must it feel like to know your own father was responsible for the death and suffering of others? How did it twist the soul to grow up in the shadow of a man's crimes? I'd been living in the shadow of my brother's death for three years now, and it had crippled us all. Kara had been living with this since birth.

I was death's sister.

She was murder's daughter.

As I saw it, I could cause us both further suffering, or I could hit the off switch on my conscience and fall into line beside her. Even if I wanted to refuse, I wasn't sure I had the willpower. Her presence was enough to sway me on most things. She replaced the oxygen in the room, making my head swim.

Besides, I told myself, they were just words. What harm could they really do? Maybe the ethics of what Kara was doing was questionable, but I was helping my friend. Didn't intention count more than the act? Like killing someone in self-defense—it was still murder, but the intention made all the difference.

The first letter was to John Willhelm. Kara praised his bravery and affirmed his innocence. Then she asked him to send her something—a token of their *friendship*. I was against the blatant flattery, but Kara insisted a little honey sweetened the pot. They were far more likely to send something she could collect or sell if they thought she believed all their hype.

The second letter was another reply, this one to a man on death row here in Texas. His execution date was set for a mere four months away. The clock was ticking on what could be coaxed out of him.

"But it'll be worth a dozen times as much as soon as he's dead," Kara announced proudly. She traded in murderabilia the way other kids traded Yu-Gi-Oh! cards. Every time I opened my mouth to protest, I thought of her dad and what that must feel like and closed it again.

The third letter was to a new inmate, one we researched together. His name was Allen Tullis, and he'd been sentenced to life without parole for a string of violent bank robberies in the eighties. Altogether, he'd killed five tellers, three security guards, and one of his own men. It was quite a body count. Such things drove the price up, Kara informed me.

Alan was known to correspond with a select few outside the penitentiary. Most of them young, blond women. We'd chosen our words carefully, sticking to questions about his crimes, his time behind bars, and his personal interests. When the letter was finished, Kara drew little pink stars in all the corners, then sprayed it with a dash of French perfume simply labeled *Girl*. She coated her lips in a heavy layer of red lipstick and placed a kiss next to where her signature would go.

"We did this one together—we should both sign it." Her eyes were wide and fervent as they found mine.

"Kara, I—" What could I say? I'd helped her write it after all. "I don't want to put my name on there. I mean, not that it's wrong or anything." *Even though it is.* "I still don't think it's safe, even if these guys are never getting out."

Kara twisted her still red lips to one side, thinking. "Then make one up."

"A name?"

"Or we could make one up together."

"Like, a whole fake person?"

She nodded eagerly. "Yeah! Or like, a band. What if we weren't just one girl? What if we signed it something cool, like a group name? Something mysterious."

"You mean like a cult?"

Kara laughed, and the sound was high and bright and full of freedom. "Like a fan club. A *following* of sorts."

I frowned. "Do you think he'll respond to that?"

She shrugged in her effortless way. "Dunno. Worth a shot. These guys are all egomaniacs. They'd probably wet themselves over the very idea of having their own organized groupies."

My eyes darted away as her words brought back last night's unfortunate events. But Kara couldn't be blamed for her choice of words. She couldn't have known. "Okay. We could just call ourselves *The Following*."

"No. Too bland." Kara leaned back on her pillows, crossing one bare leg over another. "Let's think about this. Let's make it count."

I paced around her bed. "Well, what's the whole point of this anyway?" Her eyes followed me around the room. "I mean, what are we really doing here? What do we have to offer these guys?"

Kara sat up. "Duh, Olives! We're like the Messiah to these whack jobs. We're bringing them life again, connection, hope, a sympathetic ear. They sit in their cells, pining away for the outside world, and then one of my letters breezes in, trailing the scent of distant winds behind it. They're Lazarus, and we're raising them from the dead. We're the goddamn breath of life."

I was unsettled by her passion, the altruism she carried in her words, but I tried not to show it. "Okay. So can we play off of that somehow? Like, *The Prophets* or *The Saviors*?"

"Too masculine. They should know we're girls. It makes a world of difference. Makes 'em think with the wrong head."

I thought of some of the letters I'd seen earlier and bristled, but I could see her point. "*Lazarus Girls*?" I tried again.

She smiled with one corner of her mouth. "Closer." Then her eyes grew bold as cold, blue stars and her lips widened in a silent *oh*. "I got it!"

I leaned in, ready.

"*Resurrection Girls*."

I had to admit, it was kind of perfect. "Put it down," I told her. "That's the one."

She snatched up her pen and scrawled the name next to the outline of her puckered lips.

I helped her decorate the envelopes, stuffing my doubts into them with the folded letters. Somehow, that signature felt worse than half the bad things I'd done in my life so far. And at the same time, it filled me with the same gust of life I imagined it would old Allen Tullis. Kara was my resurrection girl, my messiah, and I was Lazarus, rising from the grave at her command. But there was something unnatural in it. Was I to be a miracle? Or simply an abomination?

I couldn't yet say.

I left feeling one part guilty, one part nauseous, and two parts exhilarated.

CHAPTER 11

Sybil was smoking by the door when I came out, but she stood, shaking her head, and withdrew inside as I descended the porch stairs.

I crossed the lawn and was halfway across the street when I heard my name. Prescott was walking his dog in a pair of oversize sweatpants and a University of Texas T-shirt.

At first I froze, as if I'd been caught in the act of something shameful. Then my lips betrayed me, curving into a smile I couldn't hide. I met him under the lamp on our side of the street.

"Fun day?" he asked as I neared him. "You look, I don't know, happy or something."

Happy wasn't a look I'd worn in a while. I wasn't sure it fit now, but there was something stirring in the abyss inside me, and it felt better than the nothingness I'd entertained for so long.

I shrugged as Kara did. "Maybe."

Prescott smiled. "You didn't get in any trouble, did you?"

My mouth dropped open as I searched for words. Was it that obvious, what we'd been up to?

"You know, for the other day?" he added.

Our pool escapade felt weeks behind me already. I let out my breath. "No."

My smile slipped a little, remembering my disappointment that night. I'd been looking for attention, good, bad—*any* kind of attention. But I hadn't gotten it. Not at home.

"Good. We should do it again. You know, sometime."

"Yeah. Sure." The fluttering gave way in my chest, as it so often did around him before Robby died.

His eyes flickered from my face to the house behind. It had been only a second, but it was enough to give him away. It wasn't me he was interested in seeing again. It was Kara.

"She has a boyfriend," I lied. I didn't know what possessed me.

"Really?" Disappointment ringed his eyes, tugged at the corners of his mouth.

Yeah, she has a dozen of them. They're all convicts with records as long as your arm and body counts that would make a military sniper blush.

"No."

Hard as I tried, I couldn't *be* Kara. I didn't do off the cuff. I couldn't lie with a straight face or ooze charm to get what I wanted. I couldn't mask the scent of my betrayal with a spritz of designer perfume. I was a Resurrection Girl, but Kara was the one with all the power. I just licked her envelopes.

I walked past Prescott, suddenly tired of everything, of *feeling*.

"Olivia," he called.

I turned to look at him, my hands tucked into my front pockets, my heart resigned. "What?"

"You won't tell her, will you?" He looked nearly as young as he had the last time we'd played in the street together. How old had we been then? Maybe nine? Ten? His round eyes looked almost green in the yellowing light, instead of their usual night-sky blue. His hair was ruffled in a place or two. His face was open and questioning. His English bulldog, Samson, wrapped his leash once around Prescott's legs and looked up at me with nearly as pathetic an expression as his owner.

You're used to this, Olivia, I told myself. *You're the queen of unseen.* So why did it suddenly hurt so much? "Tell her what?"

His face broke into a dimpled grin. "Thanks."

I turned back for my house. *No, Prescott, I won't tell Kara that you like her, but I won't have to. She already knows. We all do.*

When I dragged myself inside, my dad was at the dining table, half a dozen Chinese takeout boxes arrayed before him. He turned and appraised me. "Where were you?"

He didn't sound angry exactly, but he didn't sound pleased either. My heart gave a hopeful thump. "Across the street."

"Where?" He seemed confused.

"The Hallases'. Our new neighbors, remember? You sent me over with a potted plant the other morning." Could he truly have forgotten so quickly?

"Oh." He turned back to his fare. "That's right," he muttered to himself. "That's right." His tie was thrown over one shoulder, the way he always used to do when he'd come in from work and sit down to dinner with us.

I circled the table slowly.

"Sit. Eat," he commanded without so much as a glance up. "I already took a plate to your mother."

I grabbed an open container of pork fried rice and a pair of disposable chopsticks. "Mom's eating?"

His eyes found mine then. "Is that meant to be funny?" His tone was cold.

I shook my head. I hadn't meant it to come out quite like that, but she rarely ate more than a few bites of anything. *Except that damned jelly*, I thought. For whatever reason, she couldn't wait to dig into that.

He dropped his gaze back to his sweet and sour chicken. "Olivia, your mother...She's trying."

I chewed my reply. I'd heard the beginnings of this speech a bazillion times in the last three years. I could practically recite it by heart. *This has been hard on her. She needs our help now. We have to be strong for her.* And so on. I think, sometimes, he believed it all.

But I knew the truth. This wasn't going to get any better. She wasn't recovering. She would always need our help. And the worst part was how he'd skip over what *it* was. He'd never say "Robby's death" or even speak my brother's name. It was always *this* or *it*, like my brother had just been a thing. Kara's words rung hollow in my ears: *They're still human beings.*

"...she needs time to recover," he was saying now. "It was a real blow."

I almost choked on my rice. "He," I said bluntly.

"What?" My dad put down his fork and looked at me, *really* looked at me. He'd never learned to use chopsticks.

"He," I said again. I was tired of playing dead for them. I was alive, godammit, not that anyone noticed besides the blind old bat across the street. I was a Resurrection Girl. "He, he, *he*."

My dad's mouth fell open.

"And he has a name, or don't you remember?"

A scarlet flush began to creep up my dad's face. I ignored it.

"Come on, say it with me. Rooo-bbyyy. Robby Foster. He was a person, not an *it*. And he died. It wasn't a *blow* or a *thing*. It was more than an inconvenience. It was an accident. It was a death."

"Olivia, you can't speak—"

I slammed my hand down on the table and stood up. "What? I can't speak what? His name? Robby!" I said aloud. And then again, even louder, so Prescott Peters outside and his bulldog Samson and even Sibyl in her rocking chair across the street would hear me. "*Robby! Roooohhhbyyyy!*"

I grabbed my fried rice and chopsticks and bolted for the stairs before he could stop me. Behind my locked door, I waited, heart drilling, for the knock to come. An angry fist at the door. Shouts of *Open up or else!*

I heard my mother's door click open—silence—then click closed again. But a few minutes in, I realized they wouldn't give chase, not the other night and not now. Still, the echo of my brother's name was careening off a thousand surfaces in our house and on our street. My heart was beating again to those two syllables, my head buzzing with the high of rebellion.

I ate my fried rice alone on my bed, but it didn't taste as good as the satisfaction.

CHAPTER 12

The knock at my bedroom door the next morning was the biggest surprise I'd received all summer. I opened it a crack, and Kara's heart-shaped face greeted me.

"Your mother let me in," she told me, pushing my door open wider and breezing past into my room. She sat down on my bed.

I closed the door behind her. "My *mother*?" I couldn't remember the last time my mother had answered our front door.

"Yeah," Kara answered with an odd look on her face. "The older woman that lives here with the unwashed, brown hair and the silk bathrobe? That's your mother, right?"

I nodded, blinking the sand from my eyes. "She's up?"

"Guess so," Kara said, arching her dark eyebrows like I was losing it.

"Downstairs?"

"Appears to be."

I spun toward the window. "What time is it?"

Kara pulled her cell from a back pocket and brushed her thumb across its surface. "Nine twenty-seven," she supplied. "A.M."

My shoulders sagged. "Did she speak to you?"

Kara had been flipping through a catalog on my bed. She rolled it up and looked down her perfect nose at me. "Olives, where exactly are you going with this line of questioning? I knocked. She opened the door. Then she said, 'She's upstairs.' And she held it wide for me to come in."

"Huh." Since the day she tried to tear my hair out, I hadn't seen her downstairs except for that unfortunate incident with the photo album. I glanced back at Kara. "You're up early."

She shrugged and lay down on one elbow. "I wanted to check on you. I was worried."

"You were worried about me?" I ducked into the bathroom and loaded my toothbrush, swiping it across my teeth with rapid strokes.

As I spat into the sink, Kara stood in the doorway, her arms crossed over her chest. "Duh. I heard you yelling last night."

I rinsed my mouth and wiped it on the hand towel. "Oh. That." I brushed past Kara and darted back into my bed.

"Yeah, *that*." Kara tossed a pillow at my head.

"You heard that? In your house?" I wanted to crawl under the covers with one of my mom's pill bottles and disappear.

"Pretty sure the whole street heard that." She sat down next to me. "Who's Robby?"

"Was," I corrected her. "Robby *was* my brother."

"The dead one," she said softly.

I didn't need to confirm that.

Kara put an arm down to my left and leaned over me, brushing my hair away from my eyes with her other hand. She was chewing a piece of gum that smelled like strawberries and spun sugar. "Don't be sad, Olives."

"I'm fine," I lied.

Kara pulled a folded envelope from her back pocket. "Another one came this morning. I think it's time for the Resurrection Girls to make a new friend. Got any paper?"

I wasn't sure I had the stomach for another letter so soon, but it beat lying around inside all day, waiting for my dad. I sat up. "Yeah. In that drawer."

Kara slunk to my desk and pulled out a stack of striped-and-flowered stationary. "Perfect!" She beamed. "Let's write."

I stood up and pulled on a pair of faded shorts. "Okay. But not here."

Downstairs, my mother was huddled on the sofa, the living room television muted before her as headlines rolled across the screen and over-tan men with silver hair talked from plastic faces. I wasn't sure what the point was of watching the news on mute, but it was the most interest she'd shown in the outside world in three years, and I didn't want to spoil it.

"Kara and I are going to take a walk." The words were soft and false in my mouth, like foam. I couldn't remember the last time I'd had to actually tell her where I was going or what I was doing.

She turned, and her eyes were heavy lidded though she made a show of trying to hold them open.

What was she on this time? Xanax probably. That was a

favorite daytime choice. Or Seroquel. Or both. But her face was clean and dewy with moisturizer, and even if her hair needed washing, she'd pushed it back behind a wide cotton band.

"Be careful," she said in a voice that almost sounded like it used to, like love and care and maternal impulse.

I gave her a smile—a short one, but a smile nonetheless. *It's good to see you again, Mom. It's been a while. Three years at last count?* "Okay," I assured her.

Kara stood beside me, twirling a lock of honeyed hair around her index finger and smacking her gum. The aquamarine ring flashed on her hand, but Mom didn't notice. She turned back to her silent screen.

Kara pulled past me and grabbed my wrist, dragging me along. Her eyes said, *Let's go already.*

I stood at the door and looked toward the sofa, to the back of my mother's head. How many times had she wanted to say his name herself? To scream it at the world? To beat her chest in her ragged fury and call for the son she'd lost and would never hold again? How many times had she suffered the *it*s and the *thing*s of my dad's tired speeches, all the while holding his name silently in her heart, this boy, this person who had lived and breathed and moved through life with her own long nose and crooked smile?

Maybe she hated me, hated us both, because we weren't Robby, and we couldn't bring him back. But at least, *at least*, I could say his name. And that was something.

CHAPTER 13

"Okay, girl genius. Where are we gonna go? This letter is burning a hole in my pocket."

I stared across the street to where Sybil was creaking away in her evil rocking chair and sighed. I really didn't feel like another run-in with her just yet. To my right, Prescott's house was a few lawns over. If we went that way and he spotted us through the window, he'd be all over Kara before I could spell *Resurrection Girls*. I wasn't sure I could stomach more of his sappy pining, and I didn't want to share Kara. Not today. Not after last night's shouting match with my dad. *And* I wasn't ready to answer questions from him about what we were doing, or what happened last night, or anything else for that matter. I needed breathing room.

I looked left and started walking. There was a small utility shed at the other end of our street that was used by the subdivision. I knew about it because my mom let me in there with her once when she did a brief stint with the homeowners association. Everyone called it a shed, but it really resembled a tiny, one-room house. Kind of like a freestanding garage with a front door and no cars or driveway. Prescott and I broke in there repeatedly as kids to steal light bulbs, which we then would carry to the woods at the back of the neighborhood and smash against the tree stumps. They always shattered with the most satisfying *pop*. But a neighbor saw us while walking her dog one afternoon and threatened to call the authorities. I'm pretty sure she was bluffing, but we didn't take any more chances.

That lady had a stroke four years ago, and they had her old dog put down because it kept peeing all over the carpet since she couldn't take it out anymore, so I was pretty sure Kara and I could get in there unnoticed.

Kara bounced on her heels beside me as I fingered the padlock.

"What is this place?" she asked, eyeing a wasp nest the size of a baby's fist under one of the eaves of the roof.

"Maintenance," I said. "You got something small and sharp?"

She looked shocked. "Why? Are you gonna pick the lock? I didn't take you for a criminal, Olives." She fished around in her pockets and pulled out a small metal fingernail file that folded up like a pocket knife.

I narrowed my eyes at her and took the file. "No, dingus. I'm going to do this." I shoved the point behind the metal plate of the latch and wiggled, prying outward. The screws slipped easily out of their holes.

Kara raised her eyebrows at me. "I'm impressed."

I shrugged, feeling good about knowing something she didn't. "Prescott and I stripped these screws years ago."

With the latch off, the door opened easily with a twist of the knob. We slipped inside and closed it behind us. I flipped on the lights.

There wasn't much to see. It was storage mostly, some electrical boxes, chemicals for the neighborhood pool, stuff like that. It smelled of chlorine and mold, a high, sharp scent over a low, wet one. A couple of stacks of folding chairs leaned against one wall near the corner. Kara pulled two out, spun them around, and opened them up. She grabbed a third for a surface and set it up between them.

"Voilà! Let's get to work."

I spun my chair and straddled it, folding my arms over the back. I ignored the little voice within still questioning our ethics. "So, who is this guy?"

Kara's eyes sparkled. "You're gonna like this one."

I pulled a dubious face.

She sat across from me, crossing one knee over the other. She slid the envelope from her back pocket. "Let me fill you in on all the backstory first."

"Shoot," I said, wincing at the unintended pun.

"I have three words for you—Dallas Leonard Wilde."

"Those sound like names." I drummed a thumb against the back of my chair.

Kara rolled her eyes. "They are. Haven't you heard of him?"

"Should I have?"

Kara looked nonplussed at my ignorance. "Where have you been for the last ten years, under a rock?"

I let the remark slide off me. I couldn't really speak for the seven years before Robby's death. They floated in my memory like an island cut away from the continent of my life, adrift. Or was I on the island now, watching the mainland slowly fade from view? "Something like that."

She scarcely heard me, already preparing to launch into the full story. "Mr. Wilde, as we'll call him, has a long and sordid past. He is the textbook serial killer case. Raised by a single mother who dabbled in prostitution, he was more or less neglected as a young child when he wasn't being outright abused. It's speculated that he may have been molested by some of his mother's johns, but they have no evidence to back that up. We're just going by what Dallas claims himself and what the profilers say."

"Of course," I put in, following right along.

"He started mutilating and killing stray animals by the time he was ten. As a teenager, he ran away from home, rode the rails for a while where he was likely sexually assaulted more than once. But again, that's still hearsay."

"Right. Profilers." I folded a leg beneath me and tried to ignore the burn of chemicals in the air around us.

"Exactly. So then he ends up working odd jobs in his twenties and thirties. He does a stint as a truck driver, tries his hand at logging. He moves around a lot, never settles. His relationships with women are tumultuous at best, and he has a reputation for violence—bar fights, that kind of thing."

Kara's hands moved wildly the more excited she became. I watched them flap around her like birds turned loose from a cage.

I nodded. "Bar fights. Got it."

"But even so, no one suspects him of murder. He's baby

faced, not bad looking if you're into the mullet thing. Just quick-tempered and drinks a tad too much. And when he's not picking fights with his superiors, he's regarded as a hard worker, capable." Her face was open, revealing. She wanted to know I was following along, that I got it.

"Okay. So what went wrong?"

Kara grinned deviously. Her mess of whiskey-colored waves hung dramatically around her eyes like vines, making her look a little unhinged. "Enter Wanda Briggs. A waitress at a small-town café. She is credited with being the first woman, apart from his mother, to truly break Dallas's heart. They have a short-lived but incredibly intense love affair, and then she dumps him for some welder named Tony."

"I see."

Kara leaned back in her chair, exhaling. "That does it. Dallas snaps. Wanda is declared missing a few weeks later, and Dallas skips town, but it takes six years before police find her body. Well, actually not the police, but some poor shmuck out walking his bird dog. The dog uncovers her decomposed remains next to a creek deep in the woods. They say you could tell that animals had fed on her after she was dumped."

"How?" It was a gruesome question, but I couldn't help myself. I caught myself leaning in for her answer and made an effort to sit back, be cool.

She shrugged. "I don't know. They say a lot of things. Anyway, Dallas was always a suspect, but without a body, authorities didn't have much to go on, you know? But now, strands of hair caught around her fingers match his. The police take him down somewhere near Texarkana. And when they haul him in, he starts blabbing, confessing to a whole slew of murders that remain unsolved. They think they're getting this one-time, hotshot, crime-of-passion killer only to find out he's been killing people all along. Mostly women, but a few men too."

"They believed him?" I was leaning in again. This time, I let it happen, the back of the chair pressing into my sternum.

"Well, not at first. But then some of his information checked out *and* he led them to two different bodies buried in the piney woods of East Texas. Ultimately, the authorities believe he's responsible for the deaths of over twelve people, including Wanda, but they could only charge him with three. But off the record, lots of amateur investigators and hobbyists think he probably killed at least twice that."

"Okay. So, let me get this straight. Wanda was not his first victim, just the first he got caught for?"

"His love for her made him sloppy. He might never have gotten caught otherwise. Who knows how many people he might have killed by now if he were still out there?"

I scratched my head. The way Kara told it, it was hard to separate the killer from the wounded boyfriend. I wanted to identify him as the protagonist in his own story. I had to keep reminding myself that Dallas was the bad guy. I wasn't sure Kara was making that distinction at all. "And you thought I'd love this one why?"

"Duh. Because it's a love story, stupid."

I had a hard time defining whatever Dallas Leonard Wilde held for Wanda Briggs as love, but Kara clearly had a looser definition of the term. I also didn't know why she thought a love story was the right story for me. "I wouldn't call it love, per se, but how is that supposed to make it appeal to me?"

Kara pulled a nearly empty pack of gum from her pocket and slowly unwrapped a small, pink stick. She put it in her mouth and chewed, watching me. "Because love stories are relatable. Everyone wants to be loved, Olives. Even you."

I ignored her point. "And that is a letter from him?"

Kara slid a finger beneath the seal and pulled out a sheet from a yellow legal pad, covered in perfect, tiny cursive writing front and back. "The one and only. I had to write him four times before he would respond. He's notoriously private."

"I can see why."

"Do you want to do the honors?"

I slid the paper from her hand. "You practically need a magnifying glass to read this."

"Yes, he's very precise. Which is how he got away with murder for so long."

"Right." I flip the paper over and look for the beginning, strangely taken in by his minute, tedious script. "Dear Kara..."

It felt like I was reading for hours. Most of it was pretty dry—very day-to-day stuff about his schedule and his life in prison, what he ate, how much he worked out. But his second-to-last paragraph got juicy.

It's funny you should ask that about Wanda. Most people want to know about the murders. They don't want to know about me. That woman stole my heart, and that's the truth. I guess what made me first notice her was her hair. She had the longest hair I'd ever seen, like a waterfall of chestnut straight down her back. But what made me fall in love with her

was her laugh. It sounded like bells ringing. I could make her laugh at the drop of a hat, and I loved doing it. She made some mistakes, some poor choices, but I know she loved me back.

"Wow." I looked at Kara. "I can't believe you got him to say all that. It's really personal."

"It's a gift," she responded.

I finished the letter off and folded it back carefully, passing it to her. "It's weird."

"What is?" Kara tucked the letter into its envelope like it was made of gold leaf.

"You don't think killers can love, do you?"

"Everybody can love."

"Can they though? I mean, sociopaths are supposed to lack empathy. And killers are typically sociopaths. So where does love come in? Obviously, even though he murdered her, this guy, this Dallas Leonard Wilde, truly believes he loved Wanda Briggs."

Kara let her golden shoulders slump. "Is it really so hard to imagine? Love and empathy aren't exactly the same thing. I think anyone is capable of love, but broken people love in broken ways."

I batted away the annoying, little alarm bells going off inside me and thought of my parents. We were most definitely broken people. I knew my mom and dad loved me, but screwed up as Robby's death had left us, this was the best they could show it.

Something in me shifted, the way your back can sometimes crack in a good way when you're getting up off the floor—just that accidental kind of movement that takes something so far out of place and knocks it back in effortlessly. Suddenly, the hum in my ears was gone. The little voice grew quiet. The uncertainty I'd been choking on since Kara brought all this up dissipated. Thinking of Dallas Leonard Wilde as a man in love didn't make him less of a killer, but it did make him more of a human. I could understand where Kara was coming from a little bit easier.

"Come on, get the paper out. Let's not keep this man waiting."

We wrote for hours in that shed. Not just to Dallas Leonard Wilde, but to a few other guys as well, guys Kara had been researching. She had their addresses back in her room, already neatly written across pretty, perfumed envelopes. I just helped her hash out the letters, and she took them back and tucked them into their corresponding envelopes, slipping them in the mailbox for the mail carrier the following day.

Nine days later, the Resurrection Girls received their first official letter. Kara turned up at my door, ringing the bell repeatedly until I could run to open it. I swung it wide, out of breath. "That is so unnecessary."

A dazzling smile took over Kara's face. "You're not going to believe this."

"Believe what?" I looked over Kara's shoulder, to where Sybil was rocking on the porch, squinting her unseeing eyes in our direction, like she could smell mischief. I gave her a slight nod, forgetting she couldn't actually see me.

Kara waved an envelope in my face. "We got one!"

"One what?"

"A letter, stupid!"

"Oh, right. Duh. Wait...you mean to *us*? Not just to you, but to us?"

She beamed, pointing her finger to the first line of the address. It read *To: Resurrection Girls* in all caps.

"Whoa. That was fast."

"Right?" She punched me on the shoulder as if this indicated I'd done something right.

"I mean, like, really fast." I rubbed my shoulder and tried to pretend I couldn't feel Sybil straining those cold, dead eyes our way.

"Well, they are in prison," Kara reminded me. "It's not like they keep busy social calendars."

"I guess not. Who from?" I crossed my arms over my chest, trying to deny the innate thrill I was feeling.

"That part is even better." She pointed to the return address: *D. L. Wilde.*

He sounded like a bestselling novelist that way, instead of one of America's best-known modern serial killers. "No way!"

Kara nodded furiously. "Yup. I haven't opened it yet. I was saving it for the shed."

My eyes shot left. "Yeah, sure. Just let me get my shoes on."

I grabbed a pair of sandals and shut the door quietly behind me, hoping Kara's manic doorbell ringing hadn't woken my mom. She was trying lately, coming downstairs here and there. It was a minor improvement. I liked seeing her more, having her nearby. I liked feeling like I mattered to her again. But I didn't want it to come between me and Kara. And three years of practical emancipation had made me stubbornly independent. "Come on."

We got into the shed our usual way and made ourselves comfortable. Kara had a mini-backpack filled with cold cans of soda, pretzels, and a charging cable for our phones. "Figured we should make a day of it," she said, grinning.

That was fine with me. This time, we lay on the floor on some old canvas drop cloths we pulled from a corner. "Okay, read it to me," I told her. "But slowly. I don't want to miss anything."

Kara pulled out the paper covered in the same itty-bitty cursive I remembered and cleared her throat. "'Dear Resurrection Girls...'"

I lay back and closed my eyes, trying to picture Dallas Leonard Wilde at his cot or his bunk or whatever kind of seating prison inmates were stuck with, penning this letter to... *me*. I felt giddy, barely contained, buzzing like a sack full of bees. Adrenaline coursed through me in delicious spikes. It was the feeling of taunting danger when you know you are safe, the feeling of being touched by infamy without getting burned. This man, this killer, was as close to famous as I'd ever gotten. And he was writing to *me*. To us. It felt like being seen, and that was something I hadn't felt for three long years—not until Kara came around.

I let Kara's voice course over me. It was deeper and richer than normal. Other people might not notice, but she always changed her pitch ever so slightly when she read the letters out loud. I noticed *everything* about her—the chips in her nail polish, the tiny wisps of hair that curled just in front of her ears, the freckle on her ankle that sat just above the bone like the end of an exclamation point. If Kara were punctuation, she'd be an exclamation, never a period. I...I would be an ellipsis, a thought waiting to happen, to complete itself, but never fully arriving. Prescott would be a hyphen because there was more to him than what met the eye. He was layered, not solidly, like a brick wall, but softly, like a cake stacked up on itself, mortared together with rows upon rows of icing.

I'd been avoiding him lately, staying out of his path. I didn't want to watch him and Kara fall into each other's arms. I didn't want to share either of them, but I didn't want to give either of them up. Kara was my ticket back into Prescott's life though. If I didn't make a point to bring us all together again soon, I might get frozen out of his friendship for another three to five years.

"Olives? *O-liv-i-a?* Are you listening?" She pronounced my full name the way my mother used to when I was in trouble for staying out past dark.

"Yes. I heard everything you said. Blah-blah court, blah-blah meals, blah-blah books."

"Hold on." Her eyes scanned the page. "Okay, here we go. He's talking about a woman writing him about her daughter."

"Wait. What?"

"Yeah, yeah. Listen to this. 'I've already responded twice, telling her I don't know nothing about no April Cole, but she won't listen. She keeps crying to me that her little girl didn't deserve to die. Says some private investigator with a website and a blog thinks I picked her up outside of Abilene in my truck-driving days and killed her, dumped her off the freeway somewhere across state lines. She even sent a picture this time to "jog my memory." Wants me to confess so her little girl can "rest in peace." But this girl's got coke-bottle glasses and don't look a day over twelve, and I ain't never picked a girl with glasses. And I ain't no pedophile neither. I already told the police what I know and who I killed. You confess to one thing, and suddenly they want to start pinning all kinds of crazy stuff on you.'"

I let out a breath. "Do you believe him?"

"I don't know," Kara said with a shrug. "These guys lie all the time about everything. There's no telling."

I googled *April Cole missing persons* on my phone and pulled up the picture Dallas must have been referring to. It was the one they splashed all over the media when she first went missing in hopes someone saw her. He was right; she looked young. The caption said she was eleven. Her auburn hair fell over one shoulder, and her glasses were thick, magnifying her blue eyes and making her look cartoonish. Something about the picture and his words didn't set right with me. I held the phone out to Kara. "Look at this. Tell me what you see."

Kara studied April's photo. "I dunno. A girl."

"A kid," I corrected. "What else?"

Kara looked a moment longer and then threw up her hands exasperated. "I don't know, Olives. I give. You obviously want me to pick up on something specific."

"Her hair. Look at her hair."

"Yeah, so? What about it?"

"It's pretty long and straight. Kind of like a waterfall, wouldn't you say?"

Kara pulled a face. "Geez, Olivia, that's a really specific description."

"The same one Dallas gave about Wanda Briggs's hair in his last letter to you. Remember?"

"Yeah, so?"

"Sooo maybe he did pick up this little girl. He obviously has a thing for long, straight hair."

Kara scratched the tip of her nose. "I don't know. That's a stretch. So the girl has long hair. He couldn't have killed every girl with long hair that's gone missing."

"No, you're probably right. But that detective thinks he killed this one, thinks he got her outside of Abilene. I imagine he did his research, knew what route old Dallas was driving that day."

"Maybe. Even if you're right, where are you going with this?"

I didn't know where I was going. I felt both better and worse about this last bit included in Dallas's letter. On the one hand, it drove this whole murderer thing home. These were real people whose lives he took, people who were loved by someone—someone who now has to live without them, wondering, remembering, missing. I was that person too, missing someone I could never get back. And I was broken over his loss.

On the other hand, Kara was right; she had a gift. Her knack for getting these guys to respond, and to talk, could maybe do some real good in the world. What if she could get Dallas to admit he picked up little April Cole? Wouldn't that give some peace to April's mother? What if the Resurrection

Girls could be about more than just selling murderabilia to fund Kara's whims?

"I think we should look this detective up and write Dallas back, see if we can coax something out of him. What if we can get him to incriminate himself? We could actually use this to solve cases."

Kara frowned.

"What's wrong?"

"Olivia, it doesn't work that way. If I violate the trust of even one of these guys, I'll never get another one to respond to me. Besides, don't you think that feels kind of predatory?"

"Maybe. But they're the predators. Is it wrong to prey on the predators?"

"I just think you're looking at this all wrong. You can't really trust what they write in a letter anyway, unless you can get them to tell you something you can corroborate. You'd probably just be doing more harm than good, mucking up the waters for the actual investigators."

Maybe she was right. Maybe I just needed so desperately to feel like we were doing something good here because deep down it still felt really creepy to me.

"Besides," Kara added, "that makes it all so serious."

"That's because it is serious, Kara. These guys are killers."

She retracted like I'd slapped her. "I thought we were past this."

So did I. Maybe I wasn't capable of skating over the surface of my conscience the way Kara was. "I'm sorry. It's just that I can relate to that mother he's talking about. I know, in my own way, what she's feeling."

Kara scooted over to me, sliding her hand into mine, weaving our fingers together. "Hey, don't be sad, Olives. We don't have to write this one back together, okay? I'll keep the ones like this to myself."

It wasn't exactly what I was looking for, but my eyes crawled over the knot of our fingers and I couldn't pull away. Instead, I leaned my head on her shoulder and let the tears slide down my face, dropping onto our laps in big, wet plops. Kara didn't budge. She didn't move or say a word, and she didn't wipe them away.

CHAPTER 14

The shed became our place. It was away from the crazy, pill-and-grief-induced stupor that was my house, and the just plain crazy that was Kara's, or at least that was her grandmother Sybil. Sometimes we didn't even write in there. We just sat and talked or watched stupid YouTube videos on Kara's new cell phone. The shed had a window air-conditioning unit, which ran near constantly and kept the worst of the heat and the drought away. But it still got stuffy in there, especially with all the pool chemicals stashed inside. I started cracking a back window to ventilate, but I made sure to keep the blinds tightly drawn. I didn't think anyone would notice. I guess I was wrong.

Almost two weeks after our reply from Dallas, Kara and I went to the shed prepared to read a new letter she'd just gotten from someone she'd been writing for the last couple of months. She couldn't wait to share it with me and craft a reply together, bring him in on the Resurrection Girls loop. But when we got to the door, a new deadbolt had been installed. I stood, staring at it like it was a viper.

"Motherfucker," Kara breathed.

I pursed my lips and turned to look at the nearest house just in time to see the shutters over one window snap shut. I glared at those shutters hard enough to set them on fire. "We've been ratted out," I told Kara.

"Come on." Kara grabbed my hand, undeterred. "We'll egg her house later if it will make you feel better."

"It will," I huffed, following like a disappointed toddler.

Even at nine thirty in the morning, the summer sun was spilling its liquid rage across the browning, scratchy lawns and the blistering pavement. It would only get worse. By lunch, the air would ripple with heat the way it does around a flame, and anything caught outside would bake without mercy. We passed my house, and I looked up at the tall oak that was failing us. This summer would claim more lives than I cared to imagine. Grass, trees, stray dogs, and forgotten vagrants...the young, the old.

"Christ," Kara muttered. "This summer will be the death of me."

We started down the middle of the road. "It's not hot in Pennsylvania?"

Kara gave me side-eye. "Who said anything about Pennsylvania?"

"Your mother. Weeks ago. She said you guys were from there."

Kara laughed openly. "Yeah, maybe seven years ago. We were in Georgia after that. Then Florida. But we moved here from New Orleans."

"Louisiana?" I looked down at the street as we walked. I even felt sorry for the concrete in this heat.

"The one and only," she said with a little bow.

"Why would she lie to me?" I wondered aloud, stepping around a blackened pile of dog poop.

"She didn't," Kara pointed out.

"You have a funny definition of honesty."

Kara gave me one of her shrugs. "Whatever. I don't know why she failed to mention the other three places. Maybe she forgot."

Now I gave her a sidelong glance. "Why do you move so often?"

Kara's face went strangely placid. "My mom works for herself, consulting. She gets bored. Who knows? Where are we headed anyway?"

My feet slapped time against the pavement as we passed one house after another. I was forming a response when I saw it lying in the middle of the street, legs up, curling in on themselves the way a spider's does. One wing was folded beneath it while the other stretched out, bent awkwardly to the side.

Kara stopped suddenly, her eyes fixating on its shadow. "What is it?"

"Looks like a bird," I said. "A grackle, I think. It's black like they are."

Kara looked around as if for an explanation, then at me. "What happened to it?"

I shrugged. "I dunno. Hit by a car maybe? My dad calls them 'nuisance birds.' We're probably better off."

She narrowed her eyes. "Stay here."

I shielded my eyes with one hand, and I watched her approach it with determined steps. She squatted beside it, her body blocking some of it from my view, baring the soles of her feet as her flip-flops hung down. I saw its one wing move, the stretched-out one that was angled funny. "Is it still alive?"

"Yes," she called back over a shoulder. "Stay there."

"Kara, you should get away from it. You aren't supposed to approach wounded animals."

She kept her back to me. "It's suffering needlessly."

"Just let it die." I'd had a friend in elementary school like Kara, who wanted to save every wounded ant and doodlebug we came across on the playground. I hadn't figured Kara for such a bleeding heart, but then, she did feel sympathy for the convicted killers whom society preferred to forget.

Samson, Prescott's bulldog, came bounding up to greet me, sniffing around Kara, then darting back to me again when she swatted him away. Prescott himself was only a few paces behind. He eyed me warily, stopping ahead of Kara, uncertain if I'd kept my promise from the last night we spoke, over three weeks ago. I stooped to pet Samson between his bulging eyes.

"What are you two up to now?" he called teasingly as he approached.

Kara smacked her gum, rising to walk over to him. "Whatever we damn well please."

Prescott raised his hands in mock surrender, laughing.

"Actually," I said, walking over to him, "Kara's trying to rescue a half-dead bird."

Prescott looked around us to the middle of the street, where she'd just been kneeling on the pavement. "Oh yeah? What bird? I don't see it."

I spun to where it had been only moments before, but not even a feather remained. "It was just there." I glanced at Kara, questioning.

She shrugged a shoulder without ever looking back. "What? It must have flown away."

I stared at her, trying to formulate a response, but none came.

Kara ignored me. "We need a place to hang out for a while. Somewhere close by. Got any ideas?" she asked Prescott.

"My mom's home, so my place is out. But there's a dry, shaded spot under the bridge on the gully. I could show you. Let me put Samson up first."

We nodded our assent and watched him jog back to his front door, his slobbering dog chasing behind him.

"Oh darn," Kara said in as flat a voice as she could muster. "We'll be stuck spending another summer afternoon with Mr. America."

I sniggered at her joke, but a rising chill washed over me as we began walking again. I looked back one last time to where the fallen bird had been, but the grackle was nowhere to be seen.

Prescott's troll den proved to be both dry and shaded, though comfort was apparently not on the menu. I mentioned this aloud.

"Hey, I got you two out of three. Besides, I never said anything about comfortable. At least here you'll be out of the sun and no one will bother you." He sat on the sloped concrete with his knees up, his muscled arms roped around them casually. Kara was lying back on her elbows, her ankles crossed, a flip-flop dangling from one toe. Even here, she managed to look completely at ease, seductive.

I frowned and climbed the slope to the top, stooping under the bridge overhead. I studied the faded spray paint left by scores of vandals and wayward kids who'd found their way here just like us. Messages in a bottle. *Young Thugs* in black, blocky lettering rimmed with red. *Jeremy* in a pale maroon that looked like it had once been purple, next to which some later ingrate had spray painted *sucks big cock* in black script. *Jenna T. ♡ Byron K. for eva. Tandy's a slut.*

I spun and eyed Prescott, sizing him up.

Kara tilted her head back, watching me. "Olives, you look like a cat with a hair ball stuck in its throat. What are you thinking about?"

"What did you bring to write with?" I asked.

Kara sat up and rifled through the little canvas purse slung across her body. "Two ballpoint pens, some markers, and a bottle of pink nail polish for kicks."

"Give me the nail polish," I said, holding my hand out to her.

"Why?"

"Just give it to me," I insisted.

Kara growled and stood up. "I'm not sure I like bossy Olives." But she handed me the nail polish anyway.

I unscrewed the lid, returned to the wall beneath the bridge, and began painting.

"What is she up to?" I heard Prescott ask Kara behind me.

I could feel Kara's shrug even though my back was to her. "Beats the hell outta me. I'm not Olives's keeper. These days, she's gone totally rogue."

I grinned to myself. *Rogue Olivia*. I liked that.

"How did you know about this place?" I threw the question over my shoulder before Prescott could ask me what he'd asked Kara. Let him try the hot seat on for a change.

"I come here sometimes—to get away," he replied.

I stopped my painting and looked at him. Perfect body, perfect teeth, perfect hair, perfect dimples. He drove the perfect car, had the perfect dog, played the perfect sport, and dated only perfect girls, which neither Kara nor I qualified as, I realized suddenly. What could Prescott possibly have to get away from in his perfect life?

"Don't look at me like that," he said.

"Like what?" I cast my eyes down and returned to my painting.

"Like I have everything everyone ever wanted and nothing to complain about."

"I didn't say—" I started.

"You didn't have to," he finished. "I know what people think of me. I know what you think of me, Olivia Foster."

Suddenly, I felt deeply ashamed of myself. We used to be friends, *close* friends. We dared each other to stick our arms down the storm drain and squished lightning bugs on our shirts. We sweated together, laughed so hard Coke came out our noses, and played tag a hundred different times. He wasn't perfect then. His two front teeth were missing at the same time for months on end. His knees were always scraped and bloody. His dad whipped his ass if he went in after dark. What changed? Who changed? Him or me?

"I don't think anything of you," I lied.

He sighed. "Oh really?"

I looked back, and Kara had rolled over on her belly, one arm propping up her head while she watched our exchange, deeply intrigued. "I'm sensing a history here."

"Olivia used to be my friend," Prescott said with a ring of accusation. "Then she decided I wasn't good enough for her."

I froze, my nail polish cap with brush paused in midair just centimeters from the wall. "Wait. What?"

"You heard me. You got smart and moved up to all those advanced classes, and the basketball player was suddenly just a slab of meat you couldn't be seen with."

Is *that* what he thought? My face flushed an unforgiving crimson; I could feel the blood pooling beneath the surface of my skin. "What a crock of shit!" I exclaimed.

Kara giggled. She was definitely enjoying this. "Olivia, would you care to enlighten our mutual friend here on your point of view?"

"That is not what happened. You got—got—got..."

"What?" Prescott dared me.

I flapped my hand up and down to indicate what he got. His face twisted in confusion. Jesus, did the boy not own a mirror?

Kara beamed. "I think what Olives is trying to say is that you got *hot*."

Now it was Prescott's turn to flush the color of a bowl of borscht.

"Precisely," I said before I could stop myself, only realizing after that I had basically admitted to Prescott's face that I found him hopelessly attractive. "Or something," I added a bit too late.

Prescott looked at me like he was seeing me for the first time. I tried to hold his gaze but turned away when I felt something inside shift, like those automatic doors sliding apart at the grocery store, and give me away.

"It's…whatever. You're the popular guy who ditched me, the geek. Not the other way around."

But something deep inside me cringed at the words. You couldn't divide our history between not-hot and oh-so-hot Prescott, even if it looked that way from the outside. You could divide it, like everything else, between before Robby died and after.

Before Robby drowned, Prescott and I still talked. Yes, he was changing in ways that made me flush with heat at the back of my neck and up the sides of my face, but he wasn't distant. Not yet. After Robby drowned, everything tilted hard, like a plate full of spaghetti that starts sliding off. I couldn't grasp anything at that angle, not even my best friend. I missed school for weeks, and when I went back, there was no support for the girl who'd found her brother's body. I didn't know how to reenter the world, socially or otherwise.

Prescott tried for a little while. I remember him showing up at my locker, saving a seat at the cafeteria table, but I couldn't open up enough to receive. It was easier when he stopped trying, when everyone did.

A fog of awkward seemed to fill all the spaces between us

under the bridge, and suddenly the tinkling of the little gully creeping by below intensified to a loud, incessant gurgle.

I ignored it and set to completing the finishing touches on my masterpiece.

"I come here to smoke out," Prescott said, slicing through the fog.

"Pardon?" I spun to look at him. Kara's garishly pink gum bubble froze before her lips, then slowly deflated.

"You know, pot? I come here to smoke. I can't smoke at home or my dad will smell it and skin me alive. So I come here."

"Does your coach know you're smoking weed?"

Prescott rolled his eyes. "What do you think? So don't say anything, okay? It's not like half the guys on the team aren't smoking it. It's just pot."

"Why do you need to smoke pot?"

Kara resumed her chewing, nodding in agreement with my question.

"Things aren't always how they appear. My life isn't perfect, no matter how it looks. And keeping up with everything is kind of exhausting. I almost failed three classes last year. Did you know that? My teachers only passed me because they're under pressure from the coaches, but they can only do that so many times before they get sick of it. At this rate, I don't even know if I'll get to graduate on time. My dad talks to me like I'm an idiot. My mom can't crawl out of her box of wine long enough to stick up for me. And I'm pretty sure they're both fucking other people."

"Whoa," Kara said. "That's a shit storm."

Prescott grinned hollowly. "And my last girlfriend, Becky Frey, dumped me for the Flyer on her squad."

That caught my attention. "You mean Heather? Becky Frey and Heather Jennings, the cheerleaders? You're telling me they're sleeping with each other?"

"Pretty sure they started months before we broke up."

I tried to stifle my laughter, to no avail.

"Thanks for the support," Prescott whined, but he was grinning just the same.

"Isn't that, like, every red-blooded American male's wet dream?" Kara put in.

"I guess," Prescott said. "But it's not like I was invited."

At that, I couldn't help myself anymore—I burst into tear-inducing laughter. Kara too. Even Prescott started chuckling and eventually laughed as hard as we did.

"I can't tell if you're laughing *with* me or *at* me," he said.

"Does it matter?" Kara asked, wiping her eyes.

But I said, "Both."

I added a couple more strokes to my work on the wall. "I can tutor you," I told him, refusing to look his way as I said it, my heart beating harder at the thought.

"Thanks," he said. "That would be…nice."

I smiled to myself. "There," I said, stepping back to view my work. I tossed Kara the nail polish. "All done."

Just beneath *Jeremy sucks big cock* and above *Dildo Revival*, which I assumed was either an indie band or a gang of homoerotic mimes, I'd painted *Resurrection Girls* in twelve-inch, bright-pink, glittery letters. Beside it, I added a smiling skull with X's for eyes, a logo of sorts.

"Sweet!" Kara beamed her approval.

Prescott just looked confused. "Who are the Resurrection Girls?"

I crossed my arms and grinned devilishly. "We are."

CHAPTER 15

"Let me get this straight." Prescott paced near the bottom of the slope beneath the bridge, the little gully babbling away behind him, carrying his words with it. "You and Kara are writing questionably misleading letters to a bunch of felons? Like, rapists and murderers and stuff?"

"Well, it sounds bad when you put it that way." I scowled.

"That's because it is bad no matter how you put it."

"You don't understand," Kara said, popping up to interject. She smiled an easy smile, her arms open in the air. "It's like pen pals."

Prescott glared past her to me. "It is *nothing* like pen pals. Pen pals live in an all-girls French boarding school and trade letters about what they ate for dinner and how they celebrate national holidays. Pen pals live in other countries and want to expand their experience of other cultures and languages. This is something entirely different."

"Prison is kind of like another country," I tried weakly.

Prescott looked like a disappointed parent. Kara just looked baffled at what all the fuss was about. I had no idea how I looked, but I assumed it was akin to a kicked dog with its tail between its legs. Like I'd just taken a shit on the rug.

"I think you're overreacting just a tad."

"To the fact that you are emailing serial killers for fun?"

I exhaled and shook my head. There was no persuading him. Maybe he was right.

"No, no, no. Nobody's emailing anyone. We write all the letters by hand. There's no money in emails." Kara seemed to think her logic was helping, but she only succeeded in sounding like she came from another planet.

"Money? I'm sorry. I'm lost here. Help me understand where money comes into it." Prescott, again, seemed to aim his dagger eyes right past Kara and straight at me. Why was I being held responsible for all this? *It was Kara's grand idea*, said the preschooler somewhere deep inside me.

"Kara sells the letters she gets online. It's like swapping Pokémon cards or something." My answer sounded completely lame.

"Murderabilia," she said, chiming in again, completely unruffled by Prescott's reaction.

"Kara," I said, making a face at her. "Not. Helping."

"Wow. It just gets better," Prescott muttered.

"Look, I really think you're making a bigger thing out of this than it is. Kara's been doing it forever and she's fine. See?" I gestured at her to solidify my point.

Kara grinned and waved.

Prescott raised his brows as though he couldn't believe I

expected him to take this seriously.

"They're just letters. Just words on paper, Prescott. We're not going on blind dates. Okay? These guys are *never* getting out of prison. We only write the ones whose sentences are the greatest. Those carry more value."

Prescott's brows went higher.

"*For Kara*," I emphasized. "And if it brings a little light into their bleak world, then I like to think that's a good thing."

"Are you hearing yourself, Olivia?" Prescott shot at me.

Kara sauntered toward him. "Don't be mad at Olives. It was my idea. I've been doing it for years. It's my hobby. No biggie. Some people take ballet, and some play instruments, and some take up football. I—"

"Flirt with death," Prescott supplied.

Kara frowned and looked at me. "He's hopeless. A real do-gooder, this one."

Prescott sighed. "Let me see one of these letters."

Kara pulled the one from her back pocket she'd showed me this morning. "Here, Captain Concerned. This one came today."

Prescott turned the envelope in his hands. It looked harmless enough—a benign, white office envelope with Kara's address written in blue, neat, right-slanting script. "Who's this from?" he asked.

"Jimmy Four Fingers," Kara answered sweetly.

His expression was priceless. "Seriously?"

I buried my face in my hands.

Kara made an exasperated sound. "His name is James Malloy. He was born in 1977 in Shreveport, Louisiana. He was captured outside of Dallas and sentenced to death for the murder of seven different men in towns between East Texas and the Louisiana border, each found with their throats slit in gas station bathrooms. Happy?"

"Jesus Christ!" Prescott winced. "Don't hold back or anything."

"You asked," Kara spat at him.

"Why do they call him Jimmy Four Fingers?" He peered at the envelope in his hands nervously.

"Are you sure you want to hear this?"

"No," we both said at once. Prescott's eyes caught mine.

Kara sighed. "He kept a pinkie finger from each of his victims as a trophy. Thus leaving only four fingers on one hand. One kill, and Jimmy Four Fingers was born."

"Grisly," he whispered.

Kara shrugged. "I guess. I've heard worse."

"Maybe I don't want to read this after all." Prescott held the envelope out to Kara.

"Don't be ridiculous," she told him, refusing to take it. "It's paper. It doesn't bite."

He swallowed and turned it over, breaking the seal. Inside, two sheets of plain white paper were neatly folded, covered on one side in the same precise blue script. Prescott unfolded them and began reading.

"Out loud," Kara told him. "I haven't read that one yet."

He pursed his lips but cleared his throat. "'Dear Kara, your correspondence was most welcome. I get very few letters here. Though there is the occasional draft from one of my attorneys, and my eldest sister's greeting cards on each birthday or holiday. It seems the world has forgotten James Malloy. But not you. I can't tell you how much I appreciate that.'"

Prescott stopped and looked up at us.

"They're people, Prescott," I said, echoing Kara's own words to me. "They're human beings."

"That's debatable," he retorted. "At best." But he continued reading. "'I also appreciated the online article you printed about the bald eagles nesting behind the local supermarket in Houston. Such magnificent creatures. I hope you had the chance to see them before they left. I fear I'll never see an eagle again in here. My days are numbered now. My time beneath the free-wheeling sky has run out. I suppose it's all for the best.'" Prescott eyed Kara.

She defended herself. "He loves eagles. He has a big tattoo of one on his back. Anyone who's read about him knows that. If I don't include that kind of thing, they won't respond."

"He sounds educated," Prescott said.

"He is. He put in two years toward an English lit major at LSU before dropping out." Kara was a cornucopia of facts on the criminally insane.

Prescott refolded the letter and passed it back to her. "There's more. You read it. I've seen enough."

"So you'll help us? Write more letters, I mean?" I chewed at my lip, sitting cross-legged beside Kara on the concrete.

"Write to these poor assholes who deserve to die? No. Help you find secret places to do it? Fine, whatever. It's your business, not mine."

Something about the way he said it cut deeper than anything else he'd said already. It poked at the shame welling inside me and fanned it into an inferno. "Forget it. We can find our own place. We don't need your help."

"Hey, whatever you say. Just don't come crying to me when one of these convicted killers shows up on your doorstep expecting to warm your bed."

"Fuck you, Prescott." It slipped out before I could stop it.

Kara's eyes widened.

"Whatever, Olivia." He turned to go.

"You wouldn't understand anyway," I shouted at his back.

He stopped and turned to glare at me.

I got to my feet and marched toward him. "So your parents are cheating on each other and your mom drinks a little too much and you can't pass math because you can't stop screwing cheerleaders long enough to get your homework in. You really think those are problems? You actually have the nerve to tell me I dropped you? ME?"

"Forget it, Olivia. I'm sorry I ever said anything."

"No, fuck that! You don't get to turn your back on me. Not again."

Prescott's jaw was clamped so tight he looked like he'd had it wired shut. I kept on before he could unhinge and unload on me.

"What was it, Prescott? You couldn't stand to be in the company of the girl whose brother drowned on her watch? Maybe you think tragedy is contagious, like all those other dumb fucks who dropped our family like a bad habit after Robby died." It was true. Dead kids are the modern leprosy; they render you untouchable. People don't know what to do with that kind of pain, so they keep a wide berth...very wide.

"Being who you are doesn't give you permission to say whatever you want, Olivia." Prescott's neck muscles were tensing into ropey knots beneath the skin, and his jaw now looked like he'd been sucking on a pickle for the last half hour.

"Being who I am? And who is that exactly?"

"Never mind. I'm not doing this with you." He turned to go again.

"See? Just like I said. You don't understand. You can't."

Prescott wheeled on me. "Why? Because I didn't find my dead brother floating in a pool?"

I slapped him. I slapped him so hard my palm ached with the force and his cheek went scarlet before my eyes. It should have been his eyes welling with tears, stinging from the pain of the blow. But it was mine instead.

He wasn't floating! I wanted to scream. They never float. They sink. They drift down and away until the bottom stops them, and their hair dances around their empty eyes like so many downy feathers. There, they wait for the ones who will find them, for the real victims. For me.

CHAPTER 16

We ended up writing the letter in my backyard.

After I slapped him, Prescott didn't say anything. All the fight seemed to drain from his face even as the blood rushed to it. He simply nodded, turned, and walked away.

I stood in place, trembling, with cement blocks for feet. I knew I was crying the way one knows their heart is beating, in some semiconscious, autopilot section of my brain. Kara danced around me, tugging on my wrists, speaking gently, attempting to pry me from my spot. When that didn't work, she simply wrapped her arms around me and let me fold into her, petting my head as I wept down her neck.

Eventually, like a toddler, I wore myself out.

She walked me home in silence, but as we reached the house, I was stricken by pangs of separation anxiety. I didn't want Kara to go. I didn't want to be alone. I didn't want to see my mother watching a mute television screen.

"Stay," I said suddenly into the silence, lacing my fingers

through hers. "We still need to write your letter."

Kara studied me. "I can come back tomorrow, Olivia."

I reached behind her, sliding my hand into her back pocket to pull out the envelope from Jimmy Four Fingers. I held it to my chest. "We can write in my backyard."

"We don't have to. Not today. Not now."

"I want to."

She looked down at her flip-flops, but her fingers were still entwined with mine, the band of my grandmother's ring pressing into my knuckle. There was a bang behind us, and Kara glanced back. Sybil stood on the front porch before the screen door, staring into us with unseeing eyes.

Kara looked up at me. "Okay."

I pulled her through our garage, into the yard I hadn't stepped foot in for the last three years.

I looked around our abandoned yard for a place to sit. The lawn furniture that used to sit poolside was long gone. Nobody came back here, so they'd failed to replace it. My dad paid a landscaping crew to mow and keep it up, so he wouldn't have to. Even when they were filling in the pool, he would stand just outside the door as the contractor explained everything to him, nodding. They acted like drowning was contagious. Considering how we'd been since Robby died, I guess it was. Mom was drowning in her pills. Dad was drowning in his work. And I was simply suffocating.

"You should get a dog." Kara piped up as we skirted the edge of the garage and made our way behind it. "It's lonely back here."

I'd always wanted a dog, topping my Christmas list with

"new puppy" since I was old enough to write. I didn't understand it then, but my mom had been trying to get pregnant again ever since I was born. Every year, she would take my list from my eager hands, scan over it, and look down at me with a knowing smile. "You're going to have a baby brother or sister soon to play with; you won't need a puppy."

In the beginning, I would grin and replace the bounding, floppy-eared mutt in my fantasies with an equally charming, cooing newborn. I would lay awake imagining all the baby things I would get to play with once my new sibling arrived. At six or seven years old, a baby was just another kind of pet to me, the kind my friends couldn't pick out at the store, which somehow made it all the better. But after the first couple of years came and went with no baby and no dog, I stopped believing she would give me either.

But I never stopped asking.

When Prescott got Samson in the fourth grade, I spent three hours at his house playing with them. Then I went home for dinner and cried myself to sleep.

The next day, Prescott brought Samson over on a leash. "Help me train him," he said. I remember watching them go up and down the sidewalk in front of our house, unsure who was pulling who. "I don't think you're doing it right," I would tell him. "He's not supposed to choke like that." And he would hand the leash to me to demonstrate.

By dusk, the mosquitoes were making it nearly impossible to go on, but Samson was at least using the leash without looking like he was getting a hernia. "You're really good at this," Prescott told me. "You should get a dog."

That's when I started crying.

He clearly didn't know what he'd said wrong, but he felt terrible just the same. "I'll bring him over every week," he told me, trying to calm me down. "He can be our dog."

I knew Samson would never be *our* dog, but I nodded, wiped my face, and went inside. The next year, Robby was born.

I could forgive my mom her lies.

I could forgive Prescott for having what I didn't.

Having Robby somehow made all of it okay.

Now, Kara's words stung more and less at the same time. But I was already all cried out, and I didn't feel like telling another sad story.

I sat cross-legged with my back to the garage. Kara stretched out on her stomach across the lawn, kicking off her shoes. "All right," she said. "Let's write this thing and get it over with."

I pushed the paper and pen toward her. "You write. I'll direct."

"Cute," she said, but she grinned.

We started in the usual way. How was prison life going? How were his appeals going? Kara said they were always appealing their convictions. And when that ruling failed, they appealed it, and so on and so forth, in a near endless cycle. She suggested we try and add a lock of her hair. "If it's thin enough, they'll just think it fell in there and let him keep it," she told me.

I suggested we tell him what the stock market was doing. "If the guy was into robbing banks, he obviously is interested in money."

"No, no, no." Kara sat up. "You're getting them confused. That was Allen Tullis, the first one we wrote."

"Oh. Who's this one?"

She looked exasperated. "James Malloy. The bathroom guy. Remember?" She made a swipe across her neck with one finger.

"Oh yeah, the throat slitter. Right. Got it."

Kara set down her pen. "Look, Olivia, if you're not into this—"

"I'm into it. I am. There's just a lot of them. It's hard to keep them all straight."

She was quiet for a moment while she fiddled with the aquamarine ring on her finger. "It slips," she said finally, twisting it around to show me.

"It's loose. It's too big for you."

She waited as though she expected me to ask for it back. When I didn't, she moved on. "How long have you liked him?"

"Prescott? I dunno. We've been friends forever. I think I was four when he moved here."

"But when did your feelings change?"

I shrugged. I couldn't really say. The obvious answer was when he got so painfully good to look at. But the truth was I think it started much earlier. Even before we shared a dog.

"I figured," she said, reading my thoughts. "Why didn't you ever tell him?"

I laughed dryly. "Have you seen him lately? Are we talking about the same guy?"

Kara reached forward, brushing my hair back. "Olives, you're really pretty. You don't give yourself credit for what you should, but you take responsibility for everything you shouldn't."

I froze beneath her fingers, and she scooted closer. "When you have feelings for someone, you should let them know."

She was so close I could read the flecks in her eyes like Braille. Her fingers played restlessly with the ends of my hair. I no longer knew who we were talking about.

A door slammed to our left, and Kara leaned back, slipping away from me. I jumped up, brushing grass from my rear, and turned toward the corner of the garage to see my dad crossing the living room window. He was home early.

He stopped and looked through the glass, noticing me across the yard. For a moment we both stood there, transfixed. Every moment with him felt just like this, I realized—like looking through glass. We circled each other like fish swimming beneath the ice, but we could never close the gap. The yard, the pool, the drowning, would always come between us.

Kara stepped out next to me and looped her arm through mine. Her presence broke the stare off. My dad blinked, turned away, and closed the blinds.

"Cold," Kara said.

I swallowed and ducked back behind the garage.

Kara followed.

"He didn't see us," I said defensively, knowing it wasn't true.

"Of course he did."

"Well, he has a lot on his plate. And the backyard is kind of forbidden territory."

Kara was folding our letter neatly, making it envelope ready. "You've been doing a lot of that lately," she commented.

"What?"

"Crossing invisible barriers." She looked at me frankly. "The pool. Your brother's name. The yard." She gestured at the clipped lawn around us.

I realized she was right. My life for the last three years had been bordered on all sides by unspoken boundaries, defined by all the places we couldn't go, things we couldn't say. In the weeks since Kara moved in, I'd crossed more thresholds than I could count. I was finally coloring outside the lines. But I still couldn't tell if it was drawing me closer to or farther from myself.

"What does he do?" she asked me, leaning around the garage to eye the closed blinds. "Your dad?"

"He works, like other dads."

She gave me an odd expression, and I felt contrite remembering Rhea's slip about Kara's own father. "It's some kind of boring corporate gig that makes no sense but pays well. Something with oil and gas, like everyone else around here."

Kara studied the folds in the paper she was holding. "He's early today, huh?"

"Yeah," I admitted. "Usually he stays late at the office."

"You mean since..."

I nodded.

"And you buy that? The 'office' bit?"

I'd been leaning back against the siding of the garage, but I righted myself on my feet and gave her a hard look. "What are you implying?"

Kara took a deep breath. "Nothing, Olives. I just wondered."

She wasn't the only one. I'd been wondering myself how he killed his time for the last three years. It's not that I didn't believe him when he said he worked late. I just didn't believe that was *all* he was doing. But I was too scared of the truth to dig any deeper.

"I should probably go," Kara said, tucking our letter into her waistband. "Don't worry about Prescott," she said suddenly, brightening. "He'll get over it. You'll see."

I nodded, but it wasn't Prescott I was worried about at the moment. "Okay."

Kara started past me, and my hand reached out and caught hers. "My dad—"

She squeezed my hand in hers. "You don't have to explain your family to me, Olivia. You heard Prescott. Every house on this street has a closetful of skeletons. Including mine. *Especially* mine."

Her lips brushed my cheek, and she was gone, leaving me alone to face the empty yard, the pool that was, and the shuttered secrets I was finding increasingly hard to ignore.

The next morning found me standing rigidly at Prescott's door, pretending my heart wasn't in my throat as I rung the bell. I'd lain awake half the night debating. All I'd managed to figure out was that this could go one of three ways. I could wait on pins and needles for him to come to me, hoping he would, and blurt my apology then. Or I could go to him and just get it over with, like ripping off a Band-Aid. Or we could go on like before, not speaking, not really acknowledging what had happened between us, living down the street from each other while we may as well be on different planets.

By morning, I'd made up my mind. As much as Prescott's presence burned me from the inside out, I preferred the fire to the cold, hard grave of an existence I had without him before. Kara had brought us back together, but she was right; we had a history—a flesh-and-blood connection that was ours before high school or cheerleaders or even the Hallases. I was counting on that now as I stood outside his painted front door staring at the brass knocker in my best skinny jeans and a David Bowie T-shirt that wasn't exactly cool but might be the least lame thing I owned.

I didn't expect him to answer.

I also didn't expect him to be shirtless.

My mouth gaped, and the entire apology speech I'd written and rehearsed at 3:00 a.m. evaporated.

"Olivia?" He squinted out at me and scratched his chest like he'd just rolled out of bed, which apparently he had.

"Uh, yeah."

Prescott looked past me. "Where's Kara?"

The air drained from my lungs. *Breathe, Olivia*. "It's just me."

He peered at me. "Should I turn the other cheek?"

I probably deserved that. "I'm actually here to apologize."

Now he looked like the one caught off guard. "Really?"

Outside, a dog started barking as a jogger whizzed past us. The live audience unnerved me. "Can I come in?"

"Sure." Prescott opened the door wide and stepped back.

I took one step and then another, melting into the familiarity of his entry. The marble tiles beneath our feet, the stairs to the left, the hall leading back to the kitchen and great room. The family portraits hanging by the half bath door. Nothing had changed in my absence.

"Prescott?" a voice called from the back of the house. "Who is it?"

"It's just Olivia, Mom," he answered.

"Who?"

Prescott rolled his eyes at me and closed the door. "Olivia," he bellowed. "Foster. From down the street."

A woman with a neat bob wearing a silk blouse appeared at the end of the hallway. "Olivia! Oh my goodness, it's been so long! Look at you!" Prescott's mom trotted toward us, sizing me up with eager eyes. "You're so lovely," she cooed, wrapping me in a welcoming hug. "Prescott, isn't she just lovely?"

"Yes," he admitted with another eye roll. "We're going upstairs."

"Oh, but I want to chat." She pouted. "We haven't seen each other in so long." Then, to me, she said, "Isn't that terrible? And we're right down the street. How's your mother, poor thing?"

Prescott grabbed my hand and tugged me away from his mother's questions. "Too bad," he called back over a shoulder as he dragged me up the stairs behind him. "You can play catch-up later."

When we reached the landing, he turned toward the door to his room and pulled me inside, slamming it shut behind us. "I'm sorry," he explained. "But if we go in the game room, she'll just follow you. I hope you don't mind."

Mind? Being shut up in shirtless Prescott's bedroom with him? I looked around at the mess of scattered clothes and shrugged. "I don't mind either way. It's your mom. She's nice."

He gave me a we-both-know-better look. "Olivia, that's not being nice. That's being nosy."

I looked down and nodded, knowing he was right but wishing he weren't.

"Wow," he said quietly. "That must really suck."

"What?"

Prescott stared at me like he was seeing me for the first time. "Having people only see the tragedy instead of you."

A flat, one-note laugh escaped. But there was no shrugging off how dead-on he was.

"Fuck, I'm so sorry." He was visibly appalled that his own mother was an offender.

"No, it's fine. I'm used to it."

"That's bullshit, Olivia." He grabbed a T-shirt from the floor and tugged it on over his head, running his hands through his hair a few times.

"Yeah, it is." I sat on the edge of his bed. "You want to know the worst part?"

Prescott sat down next to me, a little too close, his hand just touching mine, his skin a little too hot. It took all I had not to move away, and even more not to move closer. "What's the worst part?"

"The way they pretend to care."

He looked at his hands, leaning forward, elbows on knees. "Damn."

There really wasn't much more to say about it than that. In the beginning, when someone dies, everyone's eyes are on you. How will you handle it? Will you be strong, put on a brave face, cope? Will you fall apart, crumble, make a scene? You know they're watching. You think they're seeing you. It can be intoxicating at first, the flood of sympathy that rushes in and surrounds you like helium, lifting you up. And then, somewhere between the finger sandwiches and the wilting lilies, you realize you are merely incidental. They are crows feasting on tragedy, and you stink of the dead. You're the dinner bell, nothing more.

I shuddered and changed the subject. "Anyway, what I was saying earlier is that I'm sorry—"

"Save it," he said, cutting me off. "I'm really the one who owes you."

"For?"

"What I said to you before—it was out of line. Way out. I owe you the apology, not the other way around."

I studied him for a moment, the set of his eyes, the way he kept rubbing his thumbs together, still leaning forward, elbows on knees. He was so close I could see the hangnails that framed his cuticles. The sincerity rippled off him like heat off asphalt. He sat up and caught my eye.

"Oh." I looked away and shrugged, suddenly uncomfortable with his focus on me.

"I was angry. It just came out. It's no excuse. I don't know why I said that shit."

"I do."

He waited, a questioning look on his face.

"Because it's true."

He stared at me, stiffening.

"I've never said this to anyone before," I began, feeling buoyed by his nearness, the weight of him holding me up. "But losing Robby is the best and worst thing that's ever happened to me."

Prescott was silent.

"The worst for obvious reasons. Because my little brother

is gone and my life will forever be defined by his absence." I swallowed as he listened. "And the best because it's like a doctor's note for life. I get to sit this one out, no questions asked. Anything I do now, no matter what it is, no matter how bad, people will always say it's because of Robby's death. They will look the other way and excuse my absence."

"Olivia..." he started.

"No, really. You have no idea what it's like to go through life surrounded by people who expect absolutely nothing from you."

He laughed dryly. "That's for sure. Everyone expects everything from me—to be the best athlete, the best student, the best boyfriend. My life is one big competition, a trophy waiting to happen."

"You're one of the only people to make me feel different," I told him. *To make me feel alive.* "Thank you."

He laughed again, this time with humor. "Anytime, Olives. You can count on me to be the jackass you've always needed."

I blushed at the nickname, the one Kara had given me. And then I laughed too. "I'll get you a trophy for it."

He nudged me, laughing harder. "I can put it in my dad's office."

"Right next to the picture of you, Becky Frey, and Heather Jennings," I said, cracking up.

"Oh, that's it," Prescott said, shoving me over playfully. "I never should have told you about that."

I fell sideways onto his bed cackling, and he leaned in, tickling me in mock punishment.

I cried out, "Okay, okay! I give! Uncle already. I'm dying over here."

"Poor choice of words," he said breathless, leaning over me.

"Awkward encounters are my specialty." I giggled, catching my breath. And then I realized how close he was, his face only inches from mine. Somehow in the tickling, laughing meltdown, we'd ended up horizontal, a tangle of limbs. His breath moved my hair with each exhale.

Prescott cleared his throat, and I could feel his finger stroking the side of my neck. He'd stopped tickling, stopped laughing, but he wasn't moving yet. He stared at me, transfixed. "Olivia…" His voice was hushed.

"Yes?"

He leaned in a bit more, and I knew with a whisper of instinct that he was about to kiss me. I tried desperately to hold still, to stay calm.

And then a sudden *whoosh* blew its way between us, and he was no longer pressing into me, a cold rush of air filling the space where he'd just been.

I sat up on my elbows, seeing Prescott turn as his bedroom door flew open.

Kara stood in the doorway, watching us.

CHAPTER 17

Kara fixed her endless gunmetal eyes on us, her face as smooth and unreadable as plaster. "Am I interrupting something?"

"We were just..." Prescott began. "I mean, Olivia was... Well, she came here to—"

"I came to apologize," I said, righting myself, running a hand over my long hair, clearing my throat even though I didn't need to. I felt like I'd been caught cheating. I think Prescott did too. All the intensity he held for me only seconds ago had dissipated like cooling steam at her arrival. I remembered my place. "And to ask a question."

Kara arched one eyebrow. "Don't let me stop you, Olives."

Prescott turned to me, his brows gathered, mouth open.

"About my dad," I blurted.

He looked even more confused, tugging at the hem of his shirt.

"Er, well, not *my* dad, but yours. Your parents, I mean."

Kara took a step into the room and closed the door behind

her. Her edge had returned, and she seemed almost amused at our attempts to speak in coherent sentences. One corner of her mouth tugged upward.

"What about my parents?" Prescott kept volleying his gaze between Kara and me.

"You remember yesterday you said you were pretty sure they were both, um, seeing other people?"

His eyes hit the floor, pinned between the two of us. "I remember saying they were *fucking* other people. There's a difference."

"Semantics," Kara suggested with a shrug. She had begun wandering slowly around the perimeter of his room, picking up things, turning them over in her hands, setting them down again. A Rubik's Cube. A mini Nerf basketball. A half-gone pack of gum.

Prescott looked up. "What?"

"How did you know?" I asked, tugging on his arms, pulling his attention back toward me.

Kara folded a stick of Prescott's gum into her mouth. "What Olives is trying to say is that she thinks her dad is cheating on her mom."

Prescott studied me. "Really?"

I took a breath, let me eyes fall away for a second, then met his gaze. "Yeah. Or something. He's definitely not working as much as he'd have us believe."

Kara leaned against Prescott's desk across from us, crossing her ankles. Her cutoff shorts dug into the meat of her thighs. She was wearing shoes at least. Dirty, white Converse with no socks. "Olivia is looking for confirmation."

Prescott stood, pacing, his fingers laced behind his head. He blew out a breath. "It should be obvious. You know, they get calls they have to take in the other room, stuff like that. Does he come home smelling like perfume or whistling like he just unloaded a ton of stress? That kind of thing?"

I shrugged. "Not really."

Prescott dropped his arms at his sides. "So what makes you think he's cheating?"

"He's just out late a lot. He says he's working but…"

Prescott sat back down on the edge of his bed. "Olivia, your mom—I know things haven't been the same since Robby. Everyone knows. Do you think maybe he just wants to avoid, you know, coming home for a while?"

He was probably right, but I couldn't bring myself to say it. Would he do that? Would my dad leave me to the broken pieces of our home, of my mother, to buy himself a few extra hours of peace each week? Probably.

Kara piped up. "There's really only one solution to this dilemma. You both realize that, don't you?"

We looked up at her.

"Stakeout, duh."

I wasn't sure what I was expecting her to say, but it certainly wasn't that. I stared blankly.

"Don't look so thick," she chided. "We follow him. That's how we know what he's really doing after work. Plain and simple." She smacked her gum as if to make the point.

Prescott acceded. "That's one way."

"Bullshit," Kara argued. "It's the only way."

Prescott turned to me. "Olivia?"

My mouth was suddenly dry. Not thirsty but arid, like a dump truck had just backed up and dropped a load of sand into it. "Um, yeah. I guess."

"I can drive," Prescott volunteered. "That way he won't recognize your mom's car. What time does he get off?"

"Five o'clock." I moved my tongue absently back and forth, waiting for the moisture to return.

"Do you know where he works?" he asked now.

"Downtown…somewhere."

He said something to Kara then, and she responded. I could hear the tone of their voices, hear them plotting around me, but I couldn't grasp the words. Everyone seemed very far away. My vision was blurry, unfocused. And my mouth was still so dry. I was curling up within myself, retreating, but I wasn't sure what had set me to flight. The shot was fired, and I was running as far away within myself as I could get, but who pulled the trigger?

"Olivia. Olivia." Kara stood before me, holding out a stick of Prescott's gum. The foil wrapper came into focus first. Then her nail polish. Corpse blue today. Then the sound of my name. And just as quickly, I was back.

I took the gum and unwrapped it slowly, carefully, as though this simple gesture deserved every ounce of my undivided attention. I placed it into the desert that was my mouth and felt the rains return. I looked up at Kara. She smiled.

"You have a business card for him or something?" she asked after I'd chewed a moment.

I did. There was a small stack of them in the catch-all drawer in the kitchen. I told her so.

"Good."

She headed toward the bedroom door. "We'll meet you in the driveway at four o'clock?"

Prescott nodded. "Text me the address and I'll look it up on Waze."

"Perfect. Come on, Olives." Kara beckoned me.

I rose on cue. Took a step. "Wait. What's happening?" I touched my head between my eyes and took a breath.

"We're meeting Prescott back here this afternoon to spy on your dad and get to the bottom of this 'working late' business. In the meantime, you and I have letters to write. You'll never believe who I came across online."

I froze. "Kara, I don't know about this."

"We don't have to—" Prescott started, but Kara raised a hand, cutting him off. My grandmother's aquamarine ring sparkled under his ceiling light.

"Olivia, do you want to know what your dad is up to or not? You said so yourself, you came here to ask for Prescott's help. Or were you here for another reason?"

Her eyes were suddenly merciless. How had I never realized how dark her eyebrows were before? "No. I mean, yes. That's why I came, but..."

The truth was, now that the possibility was imminent, I wasn't sure I wanted to know. There are doors in life that, once opened, can never be closed again. And I had the abrupt realization that this was one of them. If I approached, if I dared lay my hand on the knob and twist, the force of what lay behind would blow my world wide open. We had been locked in our vault, neatly tucked away, the three of us, since that summer afternoon in June. But the stone was crumbling, and a blast like this would send gravel flying for miles and lay us bare. And I would be responsible. *Again*. Olivia the detonator.

Kara watched me. "Sounds like the decision is already made."

And it was.

CHAPTER 18

We marched across the street to Kara's house. The sun was already heating the pavement to an uncomfortable warmth that I could feel through the soles of my shoes. I looked to the sky. Rain had still not fallen. The lawns along our street were browning at the edges, crisping like pie crusts in the oven. A sign had been staked at the corner posting the new water restrictions. Sprinkler systems could not run more than three days a week. Of course, that didn't stop Mrs. Perkins, three houses from the end. I could see the spray misting over her grass from here, the Saint Augustine a pitch-perfect green like a jungle lizard.

Kara walked a few steps ahead, her back to me. She'd taken a sharpened pencil from Prescott's desk and was now pushing it through the twisted bun of her hair to hold it up. On the back of her neck, just above the first cervical vertebrae, was a tiny tattoo—a heart with a skull's face. My curiosity burned hotter than the pavement. How many secrets did this girl, no older than myself, manage to keep? I wanted to count each one. To unfold them like the gum wrapper, like one of our letters, and lay them out in a broad circle. To follow them like a map to the truth at the core of her.

She climbed her porch steps, never looking back, certain I was right behind her. And even that burned at me. Where did such certainty come from? People like Kara—though in truth I'd never met anyone else quite like her—seemed born with some inner faculty I lacked, like an extra bone or organ. If you peeled us both open, she would be full in all the places I was hollow.

She didn't turn to look at me until she reached the door and pulled it open. But old Sybil was out in her rocker, seeing with dead eyes, and her hand reached out and snatched my wrist as I made to pass her.

"Olivia, sit with me a moment."

Kara narrowed her eyes. "What are you up to, Yaya?"

Her grandmother made a hissing sound. "Go. Go!"

Kara rolled her eyes dramatically. "I'll be in the kitchen, Olives, getting us something to drink. Come in when you want to." Then she twirled her finger around her ear and pointed at the old woman again.

"You think I don't see? I see you," Sybil croaked as Kara pushed the screen door wider on its groaning hinges with a giggle.

"And close the door behind you!" Sybil called out over a shoulder.

I stood stock-still as the door slammed, watching Kara's tattoo vanish behind the screen and wondering why this house was the only house with a screen door on our street, why the front door was always open as Sybil sat outside smoking her dry cigars, even in record-breaking heat. The Hallases did all things differently. They followed another way, an *older* way that was not open to the rest of us anymore.

Sybil loosened her grip and patted my hand before letting it drop. "You're different," she said matter-of-factly.

"Pardon?"

"You *smell* different," she sneered.

I was suddenly panicked, trying to recall putting on my deodorant this morning, praying I didn't stink at Prescott's house.

"I smell him on you," she said, leaning back, grinning absently.

Did she mean Prescott? I didn't know what to say.

"Not the handsome one, with the fast car and trailing eyes." She jutted her cigar down the street, indicating Prescott's house. "Though I can smell him too."

I froze.

"The *other* one."

"What other one?"

Her brows arched. Her lips curled. "The man of shadows."

My breath hitched in my throat.

"He draws near."

"I think I'd better go inside."

"Not yet," she said, slapping a hand out to bar me from the door. "I know what you're doing with her, with my granddaughter." Her smile faded. "It will be the death of me, maybe of you too."

Did she mean the letters? Or the drugs? Or spying on my

dad? I couldn't decide if she was the craziest or the sanest person I knew.

"Don't let her fool you," Sybil said, her voice going oddly quiet, oddly normal. "It is in the nature of cats to play with mice before eating them alive."

"I'm going in." I stepped around her hand.

"I know," she said as I passed. "Once I was like her—the hunter, or so I thought. She thinks she is in control. But *he* waits in the shadows. She feels his approach and her restlessness grows."

I looked at her over my shoulder. "Who are you talking about?"

Sybil pulled a long cigar from a fold in her skirt and rolled it beneath her nose. "You should know," she said quietly. "You've met him already."

"I have?"

A crooked grin revealed the row of tiny ceramic teeth behind her pale lips. "Yesss."

She lit the cigar now, drawing a long drag as I waited, feeling foolish for hanging on her every demented word yet unable to turn away from the dread they struck in me. When I couldn't take it any longer, I blurted, "When?"

Her marble eyes found mine, egg whites with gray yolks. "Under the water."

Kara found me standing in her room, trembling. She set the tray of sodas and snacks down quickly and reached out for me. "Olives? What happened? You look like you saw the old man himself swinging from the rafters."

She meant the man who'd hung himself in this house years before, Mr. Dearing. He wasn't old. He was in his prime, maybe forty-something. Who knows why a father of four with so much life left to live gives it up? Maybe his wife was cheating, like my dad might be. Maybe his kids were rotten, like I turned out to be. Maybe he was tired of the corporate grind. Did it matter? He gave his life away while my brother had his stolen. I was there to see it being taken.

"Olivia." Kara shook me. "Seriously. Are you all right? I told you I'd be in the kitchen. What are you doing up here alone?"

I collapsed onto her bed, a heap of shaking limbs. "Your grandmother—"

Kara huffed. "Is that all? Yaya got you spooked?" She moved away from me to her vanity, picking up a comb and tugging it through the wisps of her hair that had fallen from the penciled bun. "You can't listen to anything that old bat says. Shit, I thought you were hurt or something."

I shook my head, dismissing her brush-off. "She knows things."

Kara went still. She set the comb down carefully. She turned to face me. "Olives, my Yaya is very old, you understand? She's from another country, another time. Nothing she says makes sense anymore."

But too much of what she said made sense to me. "When my brother…when he—"

"Drowned?" Kara supplied.

I nodded. "I found him."

Kara leaned in. "What happened?"

"It was summer. I was thirteen. Prescott was too. He was

just starting to…to get like he is now."

"You mean hot?" she asked.

I nodded. "I had a new swimsuit, a bikini. It was purple with little black and pink flowers. I wanted to go in the pool, but my parents made me watch Robby while they were at work. They didn't want us in the water unless they were home. I put the suit on under some shorts and laid out back by the pool while Robby played and watched Cartoon Network in the living room. It was kind of breaking their rules but not really. I wasn't *in* the water, and Robby was inside."

Kara reached for my hand, squeezing it sympathetically.

"I heard barking and recognized Samson. I knew it meant Prescott was outside walking his dog. I was bolder then, not so afraid. We weren't so different yet, even though the changes were inevitable. I got up and crossed through the living room, checking in on Robby on my way to the front door. He was watching *Tom and Jerry* reruns and playing with his plastic blocks. I ducked out the front without him ever turning around."

The tears were falling. I could feel their wet tracks down my cheeks like slug trails. But I didn't care. I had to tell someone. "I found Prescott two yards down. We talked for a few minutes. I petted his dog, tried to look older in my new swimsuit. I don't know if it was working. I remember him smiling in this way I wasn't used to. I remember feeling the heat flood my cheeks, even more than the sun. I remember him touching my arm once or twice—that was new. And I felt…I felt *seen*. It was the last time I can remember really having that feeling. I walked back to my house in a cloud of giddy girl feelings, believing my crush, my friend, might actually be attracted to me too, imagining Prescott and I together at school dances, in the cafeteria, alone in our rooms. When I got inside, I didn't even notice at first."

Kara stared at me, transfixed.

"I got a soda from the fridge and a glass of ice. The television was still going. I was pouring my drink when I looked up to see if Robby had his sippy cup. I was going to save a little for him. And then I noticed he wasn't there. I looked around the living room, calling his name, before I saw it. The back door was cracked open. I must have left it unlocked. My heart stopped, and I ran."

Kara swallowed. "Olivia, you don't have to tell me all this."

"Yes, I do. I have to tell someone. And it can't be my parents or Prescott. You're the only person I can tell."

She nodded.

"I dove into the pool to try and save him. I didn't know how long he'd been down there, but I could see the sunlight glinting off the fringe of his hair under the water and the blue of his little overalls gone dark. One of his socks had come off and was floating."

Kara moved slowly from her vanity to sit next to me on the bed. She stroked my hair, my arm, anything within reach.

"I jumped in and kicked until I was at the bottom, until I could grab him, but…but…" I felt the sobs begin to rack my body as I choked on words I'd never dared speak before. "We weren't alone."

"What do you mean?" Kara whispered. "Did someone else come to help?"

I shook my head violently. "No. Not help. There was a shadow over my brother. A shadow under the water, but I couldn't see it until…until I was down there with him."

My shoulders tremored. My heart ached. The truth was ripping me open. *When we hold on to the dead, we lose pieces of ourselves.* As I spoke, some forgotten relic of my soul floated up, tore through me, and restored itself.

"I don't understand," Kara said in a soothing hush.

"It wouldn't let him go. Not at first. The shadow wanted my brother." I stared hard at Kara, deep into those storm-cloud eyes of hers. "But there was so much , and I was kicking, and he was so heavy, Kara. He was so heavy."

"Shhhh. Olivia, it's okay. Just breathe." She pulled my head onto her chest, stroking my hair.

"By the time I got him up, it was too late. He was already gone. The shadow took him from me. I saw it."

"Olives," Kara whispered. "You were hallucinating from shock and lack of oxygen. That's all."

I let her hold me, let her rock me until I could breathe steady again. Until my eyes were as dry as the lawns outside. I'd never told anyone else about Prescott or about the shadow under the water; their response would have been the same as Kara's. But I knew better. And so did Sybil. Death and I had come for Robby at the same time. I got his body, but Death made away with my brother.

Everyone sees Death once in their life.

I was one of the few who would see him twice.

CHAPTER 19

We were due to meet Prescott soon, and we needed one of those business cards if we were going to find my dad's office and wait for him after work. Kara pushed the front door open a crack, poked her head in, and then pulled me in behind her. "All clear," she declared.

I looked around our living area and kitchen. My mom was nowhere to be seen. But something in the house felt unsettled. It lacked the usual catatonic spirit that hung over it during the long, hot days. Something was stirring.

Kara was already shuffling through kitchen drawers. "Where'd you say those business cards were?"

I sat on a barstool and rested my elbow against the cool granite. "The last drawer on the right. Next to the pantry."

She yanked it open, swirling things around, and came up victorious, a sedate ecru rectangle in one hand. "Bingo!"

"That's the one," I said flatly.

Kara's smile faltered. "Olivia, we don't have to do this now."

"Yes, we do." She hadn't been so forgiving this morning at Prescott's, but my confession had softened her. And I had since regained the semblance of composure I wore the way other girls wore makeup. The tears were dry, my voice steady, my expression flat. Like a doll version of myself. *Unfazed Olivia.* We'd spent what was left of the afternoon writing introductory letters to a few more convicts, men Kara had looked up—a derelict who rode the rails, leaving a string of homeless corpses across the Midwest; an immigrant from Honduras who killed his entire family; and a guy from El Paso who liked to strangle little girls. She was especially excited about the last one. *He's in Huntsville! That's only, like, an hour from here.* Being a Resurrection Girl helped me bury my brother's memory a little deeper. In the letters, I was not tragic Olivia. I was not Olivia at all. I was fearless. I was living. I was something *more.* Exotic.

Kara's smile flickered around her lips, not quite ready to alight but dancing with the possibility. "You sure?"

I nodded. This morning had been hard, soul-wrenching even. But what I needed, what we needed as a family, was more truth. And right now, I was the only one providing it. Olivia would shrink from truth, from the pain of knowing. But a Resurrection Girl shrank from nothing. Kara taught me that. The only way to the peaceful shore was through the river's storm, a baptism by fire.

Kara passed the business card to me.

I spun it in slow circles on the counter, under a finger. The linen-textured cardstock was probably the most exciting thing about it. A red-and-blue logo marked one corner, swirls of color that amounted to absolutely nothing. *Richard Foster. Senior Account Integrity Analyst.*

What did that even mean?

"Hold on. I'll be right back," I told Kara, who was already helping herself to leftover Chinese in the fridge.

I darted up the stairs and slowly pushed open my mother's door. The room was dark, as always. I sorted through her pill bottles on the nightstand, listening for the soft sounds of her breathing as I did so. I held up each one, peering at the labels until I found the one milligram Xanax. I shook a few into my palm, recapped the lid, slid two into my pocket, popping the other one into my mouth and swallowing it dry. I needed the added resolve. I was just setting the bottle back down when I heard her behind me.

"What are you doing?"

I spun to face my mother standing in the spill of light from her open closet. She was dressed in a pair of lounge pants and a knit top. It wasn't a three-piece suit, but it was certainly the most dressed I'd seen her in a while. "Checking your prescriptions," I lied. "Dad wanted me to call the pharmacy today on anything that was low so he could pick it up after work. I didn't think you'd be up."

She moved toward me stiffly, as though her limbs were unused to action. "I see." She slumped onto the corner of the bed. "You can call on the Xanax and the Wellbutrin, but leave the rest."

My eyebrows rose.

She caught my expression. "Don't look like that," she snapped.

I took a step back toward the door. "Like what?"

She sighed, rubbing her fingers over the bridge of her nose and both cheeks. "Olivia, I'm sorry," she said quietly. Her eyes found mine in the half-light, and they were heavy with grief and something more. Guilt? Resignation? No, it was something more insidious. Shame. "For everything."

I clutched the knob behind my back. "I know, Mom," I said as I slipped out. "So am I."

Kara was slurping rice noodles as I descended the stairs. I could hear her before I rounded the corner into the kitchen. She looked up at me from the dining table, her eyes wide over a mouthful of noodles and dripping soy sauce. I froze in the doorway, staring at her.

"What?" she asked clumsily as she used her fingers to redirect some stray noodles back into her mouth.

"You're in his chair."

She looked down into her lap and then up again. "Do you want me to move?"

Did I? He was three. He used a booster seat then, a little blue-and-green-plaid cushioned contraption that locked onto the dining chair and buckled him to it without mercy. You could still see the wear to the finish from the straps. "No."

Kara started to rise anyway, but I threw a hand up. "I mean it. Stay."

We had to break with tradition sometime. Pools, yards, chairs—at some point they had to stop being unspeakable holy relics and simply live up to their function. Didn't they? Keeping them enshrined in our memories wouldn't bring

Robby back. "We should go."

"Already? It's not four o'clock yet." Kara dropped her fork with a disappointed thud into the carton of noodles.

"It's close. And there might be traffic. Doesn't hurt to be early."

Kara shrugged and looked me up and down. "Suit yourself. Just thought you'd want to change first."

I looked down at my David Bowie T-shirt. "Why?"

She moved into the kitchen, tossing what was left of her takeout snack into the trash. "I don't know. After finding you lip-locked to American Gladiator over there, I thought you'd want to fix yourself up before seeing him again."

There were traces of venom in her words. We hadn't talked about this morning because my episode had hijacked the afternoon. Then the Resurrection Girls and the letters took over. I didn't want to go back upstairs, didn't want to run into my mom again, see her shame crippling her, but I clipped that truth back, kept it to myself. "We weren't lip-locked," I said quietly, pocketing my dad's business card.

Kara stood before me, moving close enough that I could feel her breath. "But you wanted to be, didn't you, Olivia?"

I didn't know what to say to that. Yes. Of course. No. How terrifying. How thrilling. My emotions around Prescott were a bundle of knotted cords in a dizzying rainbow of colors. Pull one and you invariably tugged on another, making the colors bleed into each other.

"Tell me the truth, Olivia. You liked it when he touched you." She traced a finger lightly up my arm.

"Why are you being like this?"

"Why not?" She teased me, holding me in her gaze like a bug caught in amber. And then she stepped back, leaving my flesh a trail of goose bumps from her touch. "Relax," she said after a minute, the tension behind her words fizzling out as she turned away. "You already told me you like him. I was surprised is all. I didn't think you moved so fast."

"I don't."

Kara cast a *spare me* glance over her shoulder.

"It just happened," I explained weakly.

"Poor Olivia," she said, pouting out her bottom lip. "Tragic even in love."

I didn't want to be tragic in anything. Her jealousy confused me, the sting of her words laced with spite. I felt angry and defensive but couldn't understand why. A sound from upstairs reminded me that my mother was up, could come down at any moment. "Let's just go," I told her, moving toward the front door.

Kara caught my arm, drawing close. Her eyes flickered toward the staircase. "We're doing this for you, Olives. To help you. Promise me that when I ask, you'll return the favor." She used the playful nickname, but her words were deadly serious and her nails were leaving crescent moons along the tender underside of my forearm.

"K-Kara, you're hurting me," I stammered.

"Promise me. Whatever I ask, when I need you, you'll be there for me. Promise or I'll scream." Her focus wavered between me and the staircase. She knew my mother was awake. Could hear us if we were too loud. She knew that if she screamed, all hell would break loose.

I gritted my teeth and leaned into her. "I promise. Now let go."

Her grip slackened, and her mouth widened into an easy smile. "See? That wasn't so hard."

I rubbed at the purpling marks along my arm. Somewhere between the scented lip gloss, deadly pen pals, and crazy grandmother lay the *real* Kara Hallas. A girl who was haunted by far more than I had ever been. And I had just met her.

CHAPTER 20

We circled another level using Prescott's headlights to read the model and license plate of a black Nissan I thought might be my dad's car. An impatient honk rang out behind us, followed by a Jaguar zooming past. We were not making friends in the parking garage.

"I told you to stay to the right so people can pass," I hissed at Prescott.

"I'm trying, but it's not easy when every third car has a truck bed sticking out three feet past the lines."

I narrowed my eyes at him. "It is not every third car."

"You know what I mean."

Kara smacked her gum between us. She took the back seat so I could look for my dad's car from the front but was leaning so far up I could smell the berry flavor of her gum. Gum was a thing with Kara, I was learning. Like skulls and serial killers.

"You two argue like an old married couple. Anybody ever tell you that?"

Prescott's eyes found mine. "No," I said flatly, looking away. Kara was forgetting that nobody ever saw us together except her. Not anymore.

"What are we looking for again?"

For someone who was so gung-ho about this stakeout, Kara was unusually indifferent as we crawled through the third level of the garage without luck. But Kara lived in each moment alone, singular and whole unto itself. That was another thing I was learning about her. It explained why her moods could swing wildly from one second to the next, why she could seem so vivid compared to everyone around her.

"A black Nissan Maxima. I don't remember the whole plate, but I do remember that it starts with *PB*," I answered her. "It always made me think of peanut butter."

We circled up another level before spotting it. There was an empty space across from it and to the right a couple of places. Prescott backed us in and we waited.

"How long do you think?" Kara asked, already impatient.

I shrugged. "Couldn't say. It's nearly five. Shouldn't be long. Unless he really is working late."

"Guess we'll find out," she whispered.

It turned out to be only a matter of minutes.

Prescott pointed. "There he is."

I watched as my father walked down the center aisle toward us, his head held high, a briefcase in one hand, a cell phone in the other. My heart began to beat out of rhythm as he neared. What if he saw us? What if he recognized Prescott's car from our street? I was sitting right in front. What if his eyes found mine? Surely he would feel me so near, as I felt the warmth of him stretching out to me across the garage. Wouldn't a parent sense their own child, the way a mother knows her baby's cry from another?

I sunk lower into the seat, pressing my back against the leather, willing myself to shrink into the shadows, to disappear like a chameleon into my surroundings. He was only steps away, and I knew he would see us. He would feel me.

Ring, I willed his phone, praying for some distraction that would force his head down, turn his eyes away.

Prescott, like me, seemed to be nervous. He dipped lower in his seat, ducking his head and covering his eyes with his hand. Only Kara didn't move. She sat perfectly still, her face boldly framed through the windshield where she leaned up between Prescott and I. She blew a garish pink bubble with her gum. Her eyes crawling along at my dad's pace, watching without remorse as he drew even with our car, walked right by us, and moved on, reaching the Maxima.

As his taillights flashed and he unlocked the car, tossing in his briefcase first before climbing in himself, Kara relaxed and turned toward me. "Well, guess that means he's not a workaholic then."

My shoulders sagged even as I righted myself in Prescott's seat. But my heart couldn't regain the beat it had known—the ignorant one it pounded out day after day, moment after moment, believing in our innocence. I realized then I had wanted him to see me, to blow our cover. I'd wanted to know we were that connected, as we'd once been.

Before Robby was born, I was Daddy's little girl. He would always pick up a bag of peanut M&M's from the gas station for me on his way home from work. After Robby came, things were different, but not like this. He had another cub in the den. But he still brought the M&M's, still doted on me, on us both, as if he were the night sky and we were the only two stars shining. But after Robby died, so did the M&M's. I wasn't a princess anymore. Now that the prince was gone, the stars had gone out.

If he had seen me, would I still be shining?

If he had seen me, we wouldn't be rolling out of the parking garage now, into the unforgiving sunlight, behind a black Nissan Maxima with the license plate PB3-R961—*PB* for *peanut butter*—on our way to the truth that waited at the heart of my family. A truth that, like a defibrillator, could either shock us back into the land of the living or flatline us forever.

"Hurry," Kara urged. "You're gonna lose him if you hang back too much. It's not like he knows we're following him and will try to wait for you."

"I know, I know." Prescott squeezed the accelerator, and his Dodge Challenger responded hungrily.

We were entering the freeway now, the same we'd taken to get here. "He's going home," I said, part disappointed, part elated. "This is a bust."

But Kara wouldn't give up that easily. "Don't be so sure, Olives. Let's see this out."

We ended up following him into a gated drive leading between two long, two-story brick buildings. Prescott had to shadow my dad's car to pull in behind him before the gate closed, but I had long since given up hope that my dad would notice us.

"What is this place?" Kara craned to look at the nondescript gray buildings on either side, the rows and rows of blue-painted doors.

"It's a storage facility," Prescott answered.

"Like a warehouse?" Kara asked.

"Smaller," I said. "They're private storage units rented out by individuals."

We watched my dad's car park in front of a general entrance, and we stopped short. He got out and went inside. Slowly, Prescott rolled up alongside his car. Through the glass in the door we could see the cement staircase.

"He's going to a unit on the second story," I said more calmly than I felt. "Those are inside. It means they're air-conditioned."

I looked at Prescott.

"Olivia, why would your dad be keeping an air-conditioned storage unit?" he asked.

"I don't know." We had a big enough house. My dad didn't have the hobbies lots of other men did. He didn't hunt or fish. He only played golf once in a blue moon. He didn't collect anything, didn't woodwork or work on cars. We'd never had a storage unit as far as I knew. Never needed one. "Pull up there by that garage-like door with the busted chain. We'll wait for him to come out."

Prescott did as I asked, turning the car so we were facing the entrance my dad had used. "Well, at least we know he's not cheating."

"You know," Kara began as we waited, "I read about this guy in Colorado who kidnapped a woman and kept her naked and chained to an old bed in a storage facility like this. He would turn up once or twice a week to sexually assault her and then go quietly back to his normal life in the suburbs. She stayed like that for months until someone heard her screaming and alerted the authorities."

Prescott looked sideways at her. "Kara?"

"Hmmm?"

"You're not helping."

She shrugged. "He's locked in the state penitentiary now. I wrote him once."

"Why am I not surprised?" Prescott muttered.

I looked at Kara, grateful. I knew what she was doing even if Prescott didn't. Whatever secret my dad was hiding, it would never be as bad as a naked hostage. "What happened? Did he write back?"

She pouted. "No. Turns out he only likes redheads. Asshole."

Her hand rested on the shoulder of my seat. I took it gently, spinning my grandmother's ring around her slender finger again and again. "Still too big?"

She nodded.

"We'll have to take it and get it sized for you."

Her eyes met mine, and there was something kitten soft in them. "I have an idea," she said, reaching over to unlock the door.

"What are you doing?" Prescott snapped. "You'll get us busted."

Kara shook her head. "No, I won't. Olivia's dad has seen me, but he didn't really *see* me. He doesn't know me. I can go in there and find out the number of the unit. Maybe the door will be open and I can look inside. I'll be right back."

She was out of the car and up the stairs before either Prescott or I could argue.

We grew increasingly uncomfortable, just the two of us, as the minutes ticked slowly past.

"What do you think he really has in there?" Prescott asked.

Whatever it was, it had to be good enough to keep him coming back here night after night. It had to be enough to keep him from us. It had to matter more than my mother or me or home. "I really can't say."

We waited in silence for another few minutes.

"Why is she like that, do you think?" he asked now, his voice stretched tight over the anxiety in his throat.

"Who? Kara?"

He nodded. "Why all the killers and death and stuff?"

Rhea's words floated back to me. *Her father...* "It's genetic."

Prescott scrunched his face up. "Really? Genetic?"

I studied him quietly for a moment. Even now, even after this morning, he couldn't catch his breath around her, couldn't take his eyes off her. He was tied to both of us, suspended between us as if we were rails. If one of us tugged too hard, he would split apart. I knew not to pull on my end. I knew who'd get the lion's share.

"You can't say anything," I told him. "Promise?"

He nodded. "Yeah, sure."

"Kara's dad is a killer."

"How do you know that?"

"Her mom told me."

Our eyes held for an unspeakable moment before a flash

of movement broke our gaze. It was Kara bolting through the door and crossing over to where we sat. She climbed into the back.

"So, what'd you learn?" Prescott twisted to look back at her, a false smile plastered across his face.

He was terrible at keeping secrets, always had been. In third grade, I told him how I stole Kate Becker's pink pony pencil set. Within two days, his mother was on the phone to mine, and I had to return it and apologize in front of the entire class.

Kara drew a big breath. "Unit 219," she said matter-of-factly.

"Did you get a look inside?" I asked her, suddenly hungry for answers.

"No." Her eyes darted away from mine. "The door was closed."

"Did he see you?" Prescott asked.

"No."

"Then how did you know which unit was his?"

Kara looked at me with a sort of apology in the way her lids lowered halfway, her brows rounding smoothly over them. "I heard him."

I looked at Prescott, then away, my face flushing. Did I want more of my family's shame spilled across his lap? It was stupid of me to include him in this. But then, it hadn't been me at all. It had been Kara. "What was he saying?"

"He wasn't." She looked from one of us to the other and back again. "He was singing."

Two hours later, the black Maxima finally pulled away. I wouldn't let Prescott follow this time. I needed to go in.

Carefully, I unraveled myself from my place in his car, putting one foot in front of the other as gravel crunched beneath them. The glass door opened easily enough, and a blast of air-conditioning hit me in the face. The stairs loomed ahead.

I breathed and took them one at a time, as I had the stairs at Kara's house so often before she moved in. I knew they were behind me, twin shadows who hung on my every move. I was fragile to one, a curiosity to the other. Prescott watched like a mother hen, to be sure I didn't shatter on impact. Kara watched like a spectator, to see what the exhibit could give her. But my focus was ahead.

I reached the top and followed the long hall of blue-painted doors, their numbers the only clues to what lay behind them.

216…217…218…

219. It loomed before me in my mind, but in truth was only a little over six feet in height. Its bright-blue paint was thick and lumpy from years of repeated layers, its numbers just as black as all the others, just as tight-lipped. I touched it with my fingertips, searching for something I couldn't define. Heat or vibration, some signal from beyond.

What secrets do you hold? I whispered in my mind.

Are you sure you want to know? it whispered back.

Kara put a hand on my shoulder. "Olivia, it's no use. We can't learn anything more today. You'll have to find a key."

"We can come back," Prescott said reassuringly.

I dropped my hand and turned away, promising to return when I had the key that would expose my father's sins.

CHAPTER 21

I had only two choices.

I could take the key in the morning, steal into the unit while my dad was at work, and return the key to his key chain that night. But I would have to pray he didn't try to stop on his way home that day, or he'd notice the key was gone.

Or I could take the key in the evening, sneak out to break into his storage unit during the night, and return the key before that morning. If I was quiet enough, they'd never miss me. Prescott agreed to drive.

I had to wait two nights before I was able to get my hands on his key chain. He kept coming in the door, keys in hand, and dropping them into a pocket before disappearing upstairs. Finally, on the third evening, I got smart. As he walked in the door I rushed up to hug him.

"Olivia, what's all this?" he asked in a somewhat concerned tone.

"Nothing. I'm just glad you're home. You're a little later

tonight than usual."

"Oh, yeah. Sorry about that. The execs above me called an impromptu meeting. You know how that goes," he said with an eye roll and a light chuckle.

Really? Did they hold it in unit 219? I wanted to ask, but I bit my tongue. I thrust a bowl of hot tomato soup toward him before he could get his bearings. "I made your favorite. There's a grilled cheese on the table."

He grinned. "Aren't you sweet?" He had his briefcase in one hand and his keys in the other; he seemed unsure which to set down.

"Here, I'll take those for you," I said, reaching out to grab his keys and setting them on the kitchen counter in the shadow of the coffeepot, where he could easily overlook them later.

"Thanks." He took the bowl in one hand and set his briefcase in a dining chair.

We chatted easily while he ate, and I began to feel a bit guilty for deceiving him. But I kept reminding myself of 219, of the way he was deceiving both of us, my mom and me, every night.

"Mom was up earlier," I told him. "She got up for a bath."

"Good." His eyes met mine, his smile not quite reaching them.

He never knew how to respond to talk of Mom, and I understood why. She'd been more active lately, dressing herself, coming downstairs, eating. Things other people took for granted. But living with her since Robby drowned was like taming a wild animal. It could be nice for so long and then, *wham*. One day, its jaws would close over your hand.

As much as we wanted her to return to her old self, the only time we felt truly safe around her was when she was drugged, sleeping.

I told him I'd take care of the dishes. When he finally shuffled upstairs, I turned on the faucet and let the water run full blast while I sorted through the keys on his key chain, looking for the one that went to the storage unit we'd found. Of course, none of them was marked *219*. But of the five keys he had—one to the house, one to the car, one to his office, one to his briefcase, and one mystery key—there were two which were smaller and shaped differently than normal keys. The first had a square head. I jammed it into the lock on his briefcase, and it glided into place, turning easily. That answered that. The second had a round head and was brassier than the others. It looked like it would fit perfectly into a padlock.

I wrapped my fist around it and darted upstairs to my room.

I prepared for bed as usual—showered, brushed my teeth, threw on an old T-shirt and a pair of gym shorts. I texted Kara and Prescott and told them to be ready. I dug up a stash of Xanax and took one for good measure, tucking a couple more inside my sports bra. And then I waited.

I sat on my bed by the window, peering into the darkness. "Tonight's kind of a big deal, Robby."

The hum of a thousand cicadas answered me.

"You wouldn't understand, you're too young, but Dad hasn't been entirely honest with us. He's hiding something."

The cicada symphony played on.

"I'm going to get to the bottom of it."

I waited, listening, as I often did, knowing there would be no reply.

"I have a new friend now," I whispered. "She's…different. But I think you would like her. And Prescott—you remember Prescott, don't you? He used to bring Samson over sometimes and he would lick your face as you giggled? They're helping me."

My voice caught, and the sting of salt invaded my eyes as tears tried to form. I couldn't say the last bit out loud.

They're helping me learn to let you go.

Sneaking out was easy. Prescott didn't have a curfew, so he didn't even have to be quiet about it. Kara slunk past Sybil on the porch, who berated her for being out "at all hours" but never left her rocker or lifted a bony finger to stop her. I could hear Kara laughing from Prescott's driveway.

"Ready?" she said, her eyes sparkling under the streetlamp.

"As I'll ever be," I responded.

We found our way to the storage facility easily; it was only four blocks from our neighborhood. But when we pulled up to the gate, I realized I'd made a fatal error.

"Shit!"

"What?" Prescott turned his stereo down.

"I forgot about the gate. We don't know the code."

"So?"

"It's after midnight. How many people do you think come to check their storage units at the witching hour? We could be sitting here all night."

"Leave it to me." Kara hopped out of the car and ran up to

the fence. We watched her in the headlights, her hair a tangle of gold waves. She studied the wrought-iron fence for a bit and then turned and motioned for us to join her.

I started to get out of the car.

"No!" she shouted. "Prescott! I need a boost."

I slipped back into my seat, a tight smile on my face. "She wants you," I told him.

Prescott jumped and ran up to her, lacing his fingers together. Kara shoved a dirty Converse into his waiting hands and hopped as Prescott lifted, her fingers grasping the iron bars along the top, which ended in dull spikes. Once she was high enough, she awkwardly flung her free leg over, straddling the fence as Prescott helped her get her other leg high enough to drop down on the other side. She landed on her ass with a *thwump* I could hear from the front seat. But she popped up laughing and ran over to the code box to push the button as Prescott crawled back into the car.

"That girl definitely has nerve," he said with admiration as the gate swung slowly open.

Was that what boys wanted? Nerve? Was that what Prescott wanted? I figured by the way his eyes danced over her form as we pulled in that it counted for something. And I wondered what made risk takers so attractive to the rest of us.

Was it that we knew they could be ripped from our presence at any moment, an unfortunate victim of karma finally catching up with them? Would Robby have been a risk taker like Kara? Would he have broken into neighborhood cars with his buddies and gotten busted for smoking pot?

Would I, if he had lived? I realized that was the real question

I had been asking over and over since my little brother died. Who was Olivia without the tragedy? I didn't know that girl, barely remembered her, and would never meet her again.

Prescott pulled right up to the entrance we'd seen my dad use and turned off the car. He looked at me, cleared his throat. "Olivia, if you don't want me to come in, I understand."

In my rush to get this far, I hadn't considered that I had no idea what I would find inside that storage unit. Once the door to 219 was open, there was no closing it again. I would know my dad's secret. Did I want Prescott and Kara to know too?

"Wait here," I told him. "I'll call you if..."

"Right. No problem."

Kara jogged up to meet us, a smile plastered across her face, but Prescott intercepted. "Hey, stay with me. Olivia needs to do this alone." He pulled a stout flask from his back pocket with a cork grip around it. "For courage," he said, unscrewing the cap and passing it to me.

I tilted my head back and took a mouthful, letting the burn of whatever brown spirits he'd stolen radiate through my insides. As the fire settled into a gentle simmer in my belly, I tipped the flask back and took a couple more large mouthfuls.

"Easy there," Prescott said, reaching out to take the flask from me. "That's one-hundred-proof bourbon whiskey. Save some for the rest of us."

"Thanks," I said, feeling the flush creep up over my cheekbones and the bridge of my nose. I watched as he took a swig of his own and passed it to Kara.

I could feel Kara's face fall as I turned and opened the door, disappointed she was being left behind. I started up the staircase. In truth, I didn't care what Kara saw, *if* Kara saw. But Prescott was a different story, and I didn't want to single him out.

Inside, automatic lights flickered on as I walked along the corridor. Unit 219 was right where we'd left it, its paint still an ugly skin of blue. I held the cold steel of the padlock in one hand as I slipped the stolen key in. Like a knife through soft cheese, it put up no fight. With an echoing click, it opened and I twisted it out of its hook, gripping the knob and swinging the door open.

The smell hit me first.

And with it a dozen forgotten memories rushed in all at once.

The two front teeth that came in at the same time. Those early months when he had colic so bad he vomited formula across anyone brave enough to hold him. The way his hands were always so sticky, no matter how many times you washed them.

Robby.

He was everywhere around me in the dark. I could smell the brand of baby powder my mom bought for him, and the lilac scent of that special baby detergent we had to use on his clothes and bedding, always keeping them separate from ours. And beneath that, a thing that could not be described. The smell of a person that runs deeper than clothes or perfume or skin lotion. The smell that *is* them—their skin, their bones, their pheromones. Something indescribable but perfectly distinct, like a fingerprint.

My brother was in this room.

I began fumbling for the light switch, only aware that the tears were streaming down my face once they began to collect and seep into the soft cotton of my sleep shirt. My breath was hitching, catching somewhere in the back of my throat. At last my fingers felt the smooth plastic of the switch plate, found the sureness of the switch, and pushed up.

Light illuminated every corner, running across the familiar shapes and colors, distinguishing one texture from the next. The first thing I saw was the changing table—or rather, the diaper hanger dangling from a knob on the changing table. The little blue sheep that embroidered the top of it seemed to be wagging their tails at me. *Hello, Olivia. What took you so long? We've missed you.*

There was his changing pad, a cradle of soft, white foam wrapped in vinyl. He was already too big for it when he drowned. There was the crescent moon lamp he made us leave on every night. And his mahogany convertible crib, which we'd already reconfigured into a toddler bed for him, still as it was the morning before he drowned, the sheets half-rumpled across the top, the polar fleece blankie he loved folded over the end.

Everything, all of it, was here, in this room, just as it had once been in his. The walls were painted the same serene blue. The rocker my mom tried to nurse him in before she finally gave up and switched to the bottle sat empty. The hamper for his dirty clothes, the wooden rocking horse he'd only just got the birthday before, the night-light shaped like a star, the rug with pictures of farm animals. *Everything.* Even the goddamn Diaper Genie was sitting in the corner.

I spun in slow but dizzying circles, seeing, naming, touching each and every thing. Remembering. I checked inside the diaper hanger and counted. *Seven.* And then I remembered calling my mom to tell her to stop on her way home from work that day. *He's only got seven diapers left, Mom. You know how much he poops.*

I peeked beneath his bed, where the rolling trays of stuffed animals and his wooden train set were neatly parked. *Robby, come on. Help put your trains up. Like this. Don't just watch me.*

I opened the drawers on the dresser and buried my hands in the soft fabrics of his clothes, all folded and arranged. Shirts in the first two, pants and shorts in the next two, then pajamas and onesies, followed by socks and underwear—which he'd never finished potty training to collect enough of.

There was only one thing in this room that didn't belong. One thing that hadn't existed in Robby's room at home before he died.

Atop the mahogany dresser that matched his bed sat a dark gray soapstone urn. I ran my finger over the engraving.

In Loving Memory
Robert Mitchell Foster
"Little Boy Blue"
April 7, 2013 – June 9, 2016

CHAPTER 22

I don't know how long I lay there, in the fetal position, on his farm-animal rug, curled around his urn. I wasn't sleeping exactly, but I wasn't awake in the normal sense. Something in me had switched off, clocked out. I remember finding the urn and taking the extra Xanax I'd stashed in the side of my bra. But nothing else.

Fingers stroked the side of my face, soft and gentle as my mother's used to be, pulling my hair back where it had stuck to my temples and cheeks when they were wet with tears but had now dried there. "Olivia?" His voice was firm but not loud, not angry. "Are you all right?"

I rolled back and stared up into Prescott's face. His blue eyes were darker than Robby's ever were, sharper, impossible to ignore. Robby's were translucent, like windowpanes stained blue, round as softballs, like my dad's. I had my mother's brown eyes and hair. *Handsome* had been my mother's word for it, for the steady way our features built one upon the other. The strong bones and smooth skin, the directness of our gazes. Good symmetry, but not exotic. No girl wanted to be handsome.

Reaching up, I touched Prescott's cheek. "When did you get so good-looking?"

He laughed. "She's fine," he said to someone over his shoulder, someone whose tennis shoes were the color of old dishwater. "Okay, up you go. Come on."

With his hands under my armpits, he scooped me up to my feet, holding me by each shoulder until he was certain I wouldn't crumple.

I swayed but held my footing.

He put a hand on either side of my face. "We were worried about you. You were gone a long time." He spoke slowly, looking deep into my eyes as he did, as though he were transmitting the meaning of his words through our eye sockets.

I rubbed at my face, knocking his hands away, and looked around, the understanding of where I was and what I was seeing flooding my consciousness again. My eyes watered anew.

"You call this fine?" a second voice protested.

Prescott stepped back, and Kara's wild hair and brooding eyes swam into view.

"I meant that she wasn't hurt."

Kara stepped forward and tucked my hair behind my ears. "Olivia, look at me. Look only at me." Her eyes were like twin storms building, violent and turbulent beneath a veneer of calm.

But I couldn't pull my eyes away from his things, his room. *Robby.*

Finally, she grabbed my chin, yanking hard. "Right here, in my eyes. You understand? Don't look anywhere else."

I nodded, my chin smarting from the fierce grip of her fingers.

"Pick that fucking thing up and put it away," she told Prescott, indicating my brother's urn with a jerk of her head.

"*No*," I snapped, pulling out of her grip. "Don't touch him."

Prescott backed away as I reached down and gathered my brother's urn in my arms. Strange that something once so soft and warm would now be so hard and cold. I set the urn back on the dresser where I found it, carefully turning the inscription out.

"Olives, honey," Kara said delicately, as though I might transform into a snarling animal at any moment. "We need to get you out of here."

I took a breath and turned to face them.

Prescott walked slowly around the perimeter of the room, like he was really seeing it for the first time. He picked up a gray stuffed elephant that sat on Robby's bed and held it up. "I remember this."

I smiled.

"He carried it everywhere for, like, four months before your mother hid it in a high cabinet in the kitchen."

"Yeah," I laughed, my eyes glazing over. "He did."

Prescott dropped the elephant. "Is this…everything?"

I nodded. "Even the drawers are full."

Kara stared at me. "Like a transplant."

Prescott pulled out his flask and took a sip. "What?"

"It's a transplant," she said again. "He took the whole room and re-created it here." She looked at me. "You didn't know about this?"

"Of course not. They sent a moving truck, cleared the room. Dad said he was donating everything of use and trashing the rest. He said it wasn't good for Mom to keep seeing his stuff everywhere. That it was only making her more sad."

Prescott started to tuck the flask away, and I motioned for it.

"Olivia, I think you've had enough."

I blushed and looked away.

"I get it," he said. "This is heavy shit. But I know that a few gulps of whiskey didn't lay you out on that floor, even if it is hundred proof. You take some of your mom's pills again?"

I looked at him and back down, shrugging my shoulders.

"Whatever you're on, you don't need this with it."

I hugged my arms around myself. "The day they came for his stuff, my mother ran outside in her nightgown and climbed into the truck, pulling everything back out again. My dad had to tackle her and drag her back inside, screaming. We gave her enough pills to down a rhinoceros so they could finish packing up and leave. She slept for three days after. When she woke up, she looked us straight in the eyes and told us we stole her baby from her. 'You took his life,' she said to me. 'And you took his memory,' she told my dad. She moved into his old room that night. She didn't speak to either of us for three months."

"I remember," Prescott said quietly. "I remember her yelling out on the lawn. Everyone came outside to see what was going on. My mother pushed me back in again, but she stayed out there, watching."

"We can put on quite a show when we feel like it." His words reminded me of the exhibition we had become. *Freaks.*

Kara grabbed my hand. "Come on. You shouldn't be here. It isn't right."

"It's my brother," I snapped, pulling away.

"No," she said calmly but with a tone that meant there was no room for argument. "It's not. It's a farce, Olives. It's a storage unit full of old stuff and a jar of ashes."

I glared at her.

"Your brother isn't in this room or these things or even those ashes. And you know that. Your mom is sick and crazy with grief and pills and what she said to you was bullshit. Because you didn't *take* anything. And memories can't be stolen by a moving truck. Only a lobotomy can do that." Kara tapped her foot, waiting for me to prove her wrong.

"But..." A few stray tears slipped down my cheeks, choking off the words.

She stepped closer, daring to take my hand again. "What happened wasn't your fault. It was an *accident*. A horrible, tragic, sick, fucking accident that shouldn't have happened but did because bad shit happens to good people all the time. And you're still one of the good ones, Olives, whether you believe that or not. I know. Some of my best friends are serial killers, so I know what bad really looks like."

Prescott and I both laughed, in spite of the weird, sad twist of fate that had us here. A girl we barely knew said the words I'd wanted my parents to say all along, though they never could.

"And this place," she continued, "is not a shrine to your brother's memory. It's a time capsule. It's a place where your dad can hide how much the grief has warped his mind. Where he can run away from everyone and everything that still needs him. It's a tomb, Olivia. It's where he comes to die."

She looked around, casting her eyes from one corner to the next as though she half expected the dead to start climbing out of the walls. "This is no place for you. It's no place for the living."

Prescott cleared his throat. "I think we should leave. It's getting really late. Or early, depending on how you look at it."

I laced my fingers through Kara's and let her lead me from the room. In the hall, she leaned me against a wall while she and Prescott turned off the light and locked 219 back up like we found it.

We walked to the car in silence and said little on the ride home. For each of us, something was lost and something was gained in that room.

The drugs filled my head with a quiet buzz, but they couldn't drown out the truth. My brother's final resting place was an air-conditioned storage unit in the middle of suburbia, which was no resting place at all.

It's no wonder we hadn't moved on since Robby drowned. No wonder my mother still needed as many prescriptions as she did the week after. No wonder my dad still couldn't accept what had happened. No wonder I didn't drive and date and hang out at the mall like regular kids my age.

We filled in the pool, held a memorial, and cleared out his room, but we never buried Robby. We walked the streets of limbo at his side, waiting for something, someone, to usher us all into the light.

A shiver coursed through me as Prescott reached over and squeezed my hand. As I looked into his eyes, my heart was struck like a gong, releasing a long, low vibration that traveled through every fiber of my body, filling my head with only one thought: *I want to live.*

I waited for Dad at the table, the keys splayed out before me, glinting against the dull wood finish. I couldn't sleep. Earlier, I'd stood in Prescott's driveway, staring down the sidewalk to that damned tree dominating our front yard. The oak that *was*. I felt I could see it withering before my eyes, like shadows receding in the dark. An umbrella of green that was now splotched brown and crisp in places like burned lace, visible even at night. If we lost it, what would shelter us from the unforgiving Texas sun?

Prescott had stood at my side. "You don't have to go home if you're not ready."

My eyes were fixed on the tree. "I'll never be ready."

Prescott squeezed my hand.

"The tree will die," I told him.

"Which one? The oak in your front yard? No way. That thing has seen a hundred summers. It will see a hundred more."

"No." I released his grip, wrapping my arms around myself. "It's dying already. My father will have it cut down before it breathes its last. There are some absolutes in life, Prescott. Not many, but a few." My eyes found his, and where his were soft and lilting at the corners, mine were cold and straight as steel. "Death comes for us all. And I will always have to go home."

Prescott faced me, and I could feel his concern mounting. "Olivia, you're not making sense."

At that, I laughed. "I'm making perfect sense. I'm making more sense than I ever have, than anyone else around here does. Except her." I nodded to where Sybil stood in the Hallases' doorway, her cigar burning like a laser in the night, watching Kara cross the dimly lit street.

"The old lady?" His voice rose with the irony. "Olives, she's crazy as a bat. Nothing she says makes any sense. They should put her in a home."

"They have," I said.

Prescott frowned then. "You know what I mean. For old people."

I smiled knowingly.

"What are you grinning at?"

"You remember when we were really little and we would play hide-and-seek?"

Prescott rubbed at his head. "Yeah?"

"And I thought that if I closed my eyes, you couldn't see me? Because I couldn't see you?"

"Yeah. So?"

"It's like that."

He put a hand on my shoulder, his brows pinched with worry. "What is?"

"Death."

Prescott dropped his hand.

"We think if we don't see it, it won't see us. We put people away to die. And we cut down trees. And we rent cemetery plots or storage units for our deceased." I chuckled to myself.

"And in the end, it always finds us. But you know what's different about me, Prescott Peters?"

"What?"

"I've already seen death. I have no reason to hide from it anymore. My eyes are open now. They always will be."

I walked away from him then. And once I got inside, I sat down at the table where I always did for breakfast, and I laid the keys before me, and I waited.

CHAPTER 23

I was still waiting as dawn made its regularly scheduled appearance, a moving show of gold and pink brushstrokes filling the window at my back.

My dad came into the kitchen moments later, whistling a low tune to himself. I watched him set the coffeepot and pull a cup of yogurt from the fridge. He was licking the cap when he finally flipped on the light and glanced over, nearly coming out of his skin.

"Jesus Christ, Olivia!" He dropped the yogurt into the sink and bent over the counter. "You scared the shit out of me."

I must have looked wretched. I'm sure I had circles under my eyes. And my skin was likely pale and listless, maybe a little green as I came down off the cocktail of Xanax and whiskey. My hair needed a good brushing. Still, I waited.

He stood, watching me, his face shifting through a series of uncertain emotions—shock, anger, relief, humor, doubt, fear—before settling into a pinched expression fraught with questions his mouth hadn't caught up to yet. Then he saw the keys.

That's when I smiled.

His eyes widened. "Olivia, what are those?"

"I think you know exactly what these are. And now I do too."

He tugged at the knot of his tie. "What are you saying?"

"Nothing. I'm not the one who needs to do the explaining around here."

He hung his head, ran his fingers through the thinning blond of his hair. Eyed me again. "Did you tell your mother?"

I narrowed my eyes at him. "No."

He sighed heavily, nodding with relief.

"But you will."

"Look, you're right. We should talk about this. But right now, I have to go to work. This is a…delicate matter, Olivia. It has to be handled carefully."

The laughter bubbled up my throat from some black recess that wasn't governed by the laws of polite company. "Careful? Delicate? Like the moving truck that hauled off every last piece of his existence while Mom screamed like a banshee on the lawn? Or like the tractors that drove through our fencing to break up three hundred square feet of in-ground concrete? Or are you referring to the mountain of pills she takes to face each day without him?"

"Olivia…"

"Or is *delicate* the way she ripped my hair from my head and called me a bitch for killing the son it took her so long to conceive? Is that what you mean by 'careful'?"

"Olivia…" He raised his voice, but mine was louder.

"Maybe you're talking about the nightmares I have that are so real I still wet my bed? Or the sleeping pills I steal so I don't have to face him in my dreams?"

"Olivia!" he shouted. "That's enough!"

I slammed my hands on the table, the keys lurching and jangling between them as I kicked my chair away. "How dare you? Enough? Enough! You don't get to say what's enough for anyone else. You don't get to tell her how many pills are enough. You don't get to tell us how much grief is enough. Especially while you hoard yours in a storage facility four blocks down the road like some kind of sick fucking treasure!"

His face was the color of the pomegranate jelly Rhea had sent home with me, and his eyes bulged like those goldfish in the tank at my dentist's office, but he couldn't speak. He could say nothing and he knew it. So he stared me down in mute fury.

"Richard?"

Her voice was soft like a child's.

I looked over his shoulder to where she stood at the base of the stairs, clutching her robe, watching us unravel.

Dad spun to face her. "Rita, go upstairs. This has nothing to do with you."

"This has everything to do with her," I countered. "She deserves to know."

"Olivia!" he shouted at me. "I said that was enough. You will go to your room and stay there until I can deal with you after work."

I grabbed his keys off the table. "Like hell I will."

His face contorted with a rage I didn't know was possible in him anymore. I had stripped away the mask he molded in place after Robby died, stripped away his composure and his secrecy.

I was seeing the *real* him now, the anger and the pain losing Robby had caused him but which he'd so carefully concealed from the rest of the world. My father looked as if he could tear me to pieces or explode into a thousand shards of himself at any moment.

"You tell her, or I will," I promised, tossing the keys his direction.

He rushed to catch them, freeing me to bolt for the front door.

As I sprinted up the Hallases' front porch steps, Sybil held open the door for me. "She's upstairs," she said quietly. "In her room. She's waiting for you."

I ran up the stairs and trembled in her doorway, a knot of conflicting emotions coiling around itself like a nest of snakes, not sure why I was there. But I couldn't stand the air in my own house a moment longer, the smell of rotting words and spoiled memories rising to the surface, bubbling up like a preserved corpse in a peat bog, permeating the very molecules around us with their stench.

And this house—this room, these women—were safe. Crossing the sidewalk onto the Hallases' lawn was like crossing the river Styx. I was in no-man's-land now. No one would follow me here. No one had the nerve.

Kara sat at her vanity, hair twisted up behind her head, watching me in the mirror. I could see the tattoo at the back of her neck, the heart with the skull's face, baring its teeth at me in a sick grin.

"Does your mother know about that?"

She glanced at me in the mirror, her eyes skimming mine. "What?"

"Your tattoo."

Her fingers danced up behind her neck, grazing the inked skin the way a mother caresses the round of her child's cheek and the slope of its nose. Her eyes were far away from me for a second, registering a reality I didn't understand.

"Kara?"

Just as quickly, she cleared her throat, dropped her hand, blinked twice, and leveled her brows. "Of course she does. We keep no secrets here."

I doubted she was lying. And in the same breath, I doubted she was telling the truth.

"Come in and close the door, Olives. You're creeping me out, standing there like that."

I did as she suggested and sunk onto her bed, folding my legs against my chest and wrapping my arms around my knees, as though I could barricade my heart behind them.

"So?" Kara resumed whatever she'd been doing before I came, an open bottle of nail polish and a piece of paper before her. "How'd it go?"

I cringed at the memory of his face, shiny red and angry, swelling with all the things he couldn't say, an abscess of emotion.

Kara watched me before shifting her focus onto whatever she was painting on the paper with her nail polish. She shrugged. "You knew he wouldn't be happy about it."

"Yes."

"Would you take it back?" she asked without looking up. "Go back to not knowing what lay behind that door?"

I rocked onto my heels, thinking. An ugly truth is better than a pretty lie. Although our lies were never very pretty. The energy required to maintain a state of falsity, to resist the truth, was enormous. It was a price I could no longer afford. Even if my dad could go on paying it. "No."

I could see her grinning though she still didn't look away from the paper. "Excellent. Regret is a waste of energy. That's what I always say."

Her nod of approval didn't help shake the emotions rippling through me. Confirmation that I'd done the right thing didn't make doing it any easier. And my dad wasn't the only one fighting a barely repressed rage. My anger prowled beneath my skin like a pacing tiger in a too-small cage—anger at my dad. At my mom. At Robby. At myself. And there was nowhere to put it. No way to safely rehabilitate it and loose it into the wild, away from civilization. It just simmered under a skim of calm threatening to turn like heated milk.

And I was devastated. I could feel my chest caving in on itself like someone punching a hole through papier-mâché. I felt betrayed by my own family, my own father. This secret was so much worse than a nameless mistress. As if he had been keeping the living, breathing Robby from us and not just his urn and bedroom furniture.

"There!" she exclaimed, putting the finishing touches on her work of art. She lifted the paper by its corners for me to see. The top half was written in ballpoint pen—the end of a letter. The bottom half was a hot-pink-and-radioactive-green script spelling *Resurrection Girls* with a skull and crossbones next to it. "You were my inspiration. It has to dry before I can fold it," she beamed.

"Kara, who is that to?"

"New guy." She waggled her brows. "Total freak, if you ask me. Kills young women and eats them after. Or part of them anyway. He loves blonds. He's totally into us."

"You've been sending letters without me?"

"Duh, Olives. You can't be here twenty-four-seven. I get bored."

"And you sign my name?"

"Not *your* name, silly. *Our* name."

"You shouldn't do that without asking me."

Her dark brows flattened over thunderous eyes. "Don't get all proprietary on me. It's not like you have a copyright."

"I just mean I don't think we should be writing cannibals. We have to draw the line somewhere."

Kara sighed. "I see no lines, Olivia. Or haven't you figured that out already?"

Her tone was resigned, frank. The girlish spark had left her voice, and for a split-second, I thought I was seeing the *real* Kara, a self-aware version who knew better but couldn't help herself.

"I have."

She looked at me, a question in her heavy eyes.

I knew Kara was the sort who believed a line was drawn to be crossed and a rule made to be broken. And for a while, I liked living that mantra beside her, when it felt exhilarating but still safe, like a roller-coaster ride. Writing the letters was the drop of my stomach as the track would dip—I always knew we'd come back up, level out. But this ride was starting to make me queasy, because Kara never intended to get off, and every plunge seemed to take us deeper. I wasn't like Kara. I saw lines. I drew them. This was one.

"Why do you do this?" I asked. "Really? All the letters to killers. You say it's for money, but I haven't seen you sell a thing." Sudden dawning swam over me. "You're not doing this for the money, are you? You're a collector."

Kara stood, gazing down on me. "I want to show you something."

She disappeared into her closet, and I could hear her rummaging through things until she emerged again, a worn envelope in one hand.

"Another letter?"

She pursed her lips. "Not just any old letter." She reached inside and pulled two folded sheets of paper out, their creases worn so thin from folding and unfolding I could see the light through them. Kara had obviously read this letter countless times. "This one's from a man who was executed last year."

"What's his name?"

She smiled slightly, a little exhale escaping as she did. Her eyes rolled over the lines of script with a tenderness I rarely saw in her. "His name doesn't matter. What matters is that he and I started corresponding about six months before he died."

"Okay. So?"

She refolded the paper and looked down at me. "So? So, I was there, Olivia. When he died, it was my voice in his head comforting him, telling him everything would be all right."

"You weren't *there* there, right? You just mean—"

"I mean that I was the one he confided his feelings to as his death approached, his fears and regrets. I was his confessor. I was the one who saw him through the worst and darkest time of his life. Can you understand that? We aren't born alone. No one. We each have a mother to usher us into this world. She is the passage through which we enter life."

I gaped at her.

"Well, neither should we die alone. Everyone deserves to have someone at the end to hold their hand as they prepare to enter the passage that will carry them out of this world forever. Don't you think?"

"You're telling me you write them so that if and when they die, you get a front row seat, figuratively speaking? Do you have any idea how morbid that sounds?"

Kara shook her head, replacing the paper in the envelope and setting the letter on her vanity. "You don't get it. We all go through difficulties in life, but there's always something or someone that gets us through it. For these men, *I* get to be that someone. It's not about being a spectator. It's about being a guide of sorts."

I stared up at her, mouth hanging open. "These men are *murderers*, Kara. Why do you care so much? It doesn't have to be you."

"Yes, it does," she said quietly. She moved next to me on the bed, a brush in her right hand. Her fingers prodded me to turn around. I unfolded my legs, turning my back to her. As the plastic bristles began to detangle my long, dark hair, she went on.

"Tell me something you've noticed about us, about my family."

I shrugged. "You're different."

"How?"

"Lots of ways."

"Name some."

I hesitated. It was like having someone ask you if their butt looked big in those jeans. Wasn't it obvious? Did she really need to hear it from someone else?

"Go on, Olives. Nothing you say will surprise me."

Still, I waited. I had seen another Kara in my house only a day ago. A desperate, exacting doppelgänger who could be ruthless and unpredictable. And this felt like a trap.

"Or offend me," she added, giving my hair a playful tug. "Come on, Olivia. Humor me."

I realized she would not let up until I played along. And I'd been humoring her ever since she moved in here. Why should this be any different? "Your grandmother is blind but sees more than anyone else."

The brush made a long sweep down my hair, caressing the back of my head. Tingles swept across my scalp as I felt the tension of my confrontation with my dad begin to recede. "What else?"

"Your mother has money but doesn't work. At least, I never see her working."

Kara placed the bristles just above my right ear, pulling back and down in a delicious arc. "And?"

"There're no men."

"There never have been," she said, her voice as whisper

soft as the sound of the brush parting my hair. "For as many generations back as my yaya can recall, there are no men. No husbands, no brothers…"

"No fathers?" I asked, my skin prickling as she stroked my hair.

"Oh, I have a father," she said. "One I'll never see."

"Lots of parents get divorced. Lots of dads walk out on their families."

"He didn't walk out," Kara said, correcting me. "He was never a part of our family." She sighed, putting the brush down and running her fingers through my hair, like knives slipping through silk. "Do you believe in curses, Olivia?"

"Like witches give?"

"No. Older. Deeper. Like generational curses."

I shrugged. "I've never thought about it."

"The Hallases are a curse." Her voice was barely audible, the sound of breath blowing out a candle. I almost missed it.

"You're saying someone cursed you?"

Kara dropped her hands into her lap, and I slowly spun around to face her. "I'm saying we *are* a living, breathing curse."

Her brows had flattened over her eyes matter-of-factly, the blue-gray of her irises as tender as a bruise. A fringe of blond waves had escaped her clip, framing her face like feathers. Her lips were parted, petal pink. Innocence crawled over her like moths in the dark. "I'm not like you, Olivia. *We're* not like you. We're something else entirely."

Fear pushed up from underneath, hot and idle. "I don't understand."

"I know you don't," she said, her voice dropping an octave.

"I barely do myself."

"And the letters? The killers? All of that *being their guide* nonsense. They're part of this curse somehow?"

"Yes, in a way. They're a compulsion."

"You're saying this curse compels you?"

Kara leaned in, shaking her head. Her eyes dropped their youthful vulnerability in favor of an eager light sparking like a live wire. "*Death*, Olivia, is what compels me. Death is my curse."

Before I could form words or even thoughts, before her words could sink in and take root and grow a reply, her lips were on mine, soft yet unyielding like sticky, sweet pillows against my own. Her fragrance filled my head with strawberry blossoms and caramel, and I found myself caving against her need with a matching hunger. My fingers tangled in the fringe of escaping hair at her neck, and I pressed my body into hers, unable to get close enough. Her tongue rolled over mine as her hands wandered over my hips, my thighs, my waist, my breasts.

And all the cavities within me filled with a singular vibration, one note reverberating through the hollows left by my pain—*Kara*.

CHAPTER 24

There are a thousand kinds of pain. We don't have names for them all, but we know them individually, each by its own unique ache. We know a toothache from a stomachache, just as we know a broken arm from a broken heart.

Love is like this. There are infinite varieties of love. More than we can ever experience in one lifetime. We don't have names for them all, but we know them individually, each by its own unique ache. Love is the longing of the heart for that which lies outside its grasp. I loved and mourned my brother with spaces in my heart that were completely separate and yet forever connected. I loved and grieved my parents with another piece entirely. And Prescott with yet another.

And now, Kara had carved her own hollow within my heart, teaching me about a love I'd never known was possible before. I loved Kara and Prescott in ways that were much the same and yet totally different—the way identical twins can look the same and still be two wholly separate people. I loved

Kara like Adam loved his rib in Eve, like Narcissus loved his reflection. I loved her as if she had been shaped out of my own soul and given back to me.

My lips were numb from the pressure of this new sensation, as she had pressed her mouth to mine. And my heart was squeezing itself into the spaces between them all—Robby, my dad, my mom, Prescott, and now Kara—with a desperate cloying that left me breathless.

I was only sixteen, and I'd already known more ways to love and to hurt than I could bear.

I slipped out of the Hallases' house unnoticed. Past the bright kitchen, where I could hear Rhea humming to herself and smell something warm and rich with spices baking in the oven. Past the front room, where Sybil sat hunched in her chair, still as a cadaver, her all-too-seeing eyes closed for once. I was nearly to my own front yard when Prescott's voice pulled me up short.

"Hey, Olivia. I was coming to check on you."

I turned to see him jogging up the sidewalk, Samson at his heels. I folded my arms over my chest, feeling much too raw for this encounter. "I'm fine, really."

He came to a stop in front of me, just a tad too close, the heat of him invading my personal space. His eyebrows lifted in question. "After all that last night? You expect me to walk away with 'fine'?"

I sighed. "Prescott, I know you mean well, but I'm really tired. I've had no sleep. Too much has happened in the last twenty-four hours for me to process it all. I just want to go to bed."

He looked me over, suspicious. His eyes darted to Kara's front door. "You were at Kara's?"

I shrugged, feeling guilty for something I couldn't put my finger on. "Yeah. We talked. She calmed me down."

He sighed. "So you did confront your dad then?"

I nodded. "Yeah. I had to."

"I get it."

He didn't ask how my dad responded because it was apparent. And he wasn't looking for lurid details to feed a craving for drama. He simply wrapped his arms around me in a bear hug, his face tucked into my neck, his breath soft on my skin.

In the first second, I froze. By the third, I was beginning to lean into him. By the fifth, the tears rolled freely, releasing the feelings I had no words for. When he finally pulled back, his T-shirt was dark where I'd cried on his shoulder.

I wiped quickly at my face, ashamed.

Prescott lifted my chin and looked down at me with earnest affection. "Olivia, please don't hide from me anymore. I know what happened to you, to your family, was hard. I know it seems like we've headed in opposite directions. I know we're not kids anymore, and our relationship will be different. But I've realized something this summer that I can't shake now. I *miss* you."

He kissed me gently on the forehead and took a step back.

I looked past what everyone else sees when they look at Prescott—the veneer of attraction, something refined and practiced—and saw the boy I once knew standing before me, the one who wanted to share his dog. The one who found me the day the ambulance came for my brother, leaning against the giant oak in our front yard for support as I wailed, and held me until my parents arrived, refusing to let go until the police dragged him away. I couldn't look at him after that. I couldn't stand knowing that my shifting feelings for him had been part of losing Robby. I couldn't stand remembering how my body had trembled against his until they pulled us apart. Eventually, when I finally let myself look at Prescott Peters again, I only saw what everyone else did.

But now, I saw so much more.

And I wondered if this is what it was like to be Sybil.

"Okay," I told him, giving a weak smile. "But right now, I have to rest."

He nodded, grinning. "Yeah, okay. But come find me when you're better. I want us to...hang out. *Just* us. Like before. We'll go do something to take your mind off of all this. I'll take you to a movie or something. So come find me."

My heart, already motion sick from all that had passed over the last day, gave a little flutter. "I will," I promised him. And I meant it.

Inside, my mom stood in the kitchen, distracted, picking at a scab on her right arm. Her robe was untied, her eyes red and weary, her hair partially combed. The television was set to the news. A slick-haired reporter with a fake tan stood in front of a field of dry, brown weeds with a gleeful smile, voicing a false concern over the worsening drought.

"Mom?"

She looked up at me, a tight smile breaking across her face. "Olivia. Thank goodness. I didn't know where you were. I was going to come look for you. I—"

"I'm here," I told her, basking in the rare show of concern, though I doubted she would really have ventured out to find me. "I was just across the street."

"We need to talk, honey," she said. "Sit down."

I held my ground. "Are you all right? You don't look well. Should I get your medicine?" More like *poison*, but we'd insisted on keeping up the illusion of healing for everyone's sake—no point in stopping now.

"No," she said too quickly. "Not for this. I want to speak with you first, while I'm…while I'm clear."

I nodded and pulled out a dining chair. She didn't look clear, but the agitation I saw in her, the reddened eyes and fresh scab, those were signs she'd gone off her meds, was past due for a dose. It was a valiant effort, even if it didn't look it.

She sat across from me, tucking her hands in her lap, rocking gently.

"Did he tell you?" I began for her, knowing this was about the confrontation she'd witnessed.

She shook her head. "No. I wouldn't let him."

"But why?" My voice rose, the anger bubbling higher.

"Whatever it is," she told me, her eyes pleading behind their pink rims, "I don't want to know."

A noise halfway between a laugh and a sob emerged from my throat. "Of course you don't."

She shook her head as though to clear it. "Olivia, please. You must listen to me. I know that whatever he's hiding, it's because of your brother. We all cope in different ways."

"Or don't cope at all," I spat.

She took a deep breath. "Maybe I, *we*, deserve that. What I'm trying to say is that I don't think I can bear it. There is a fog that I am only just emerging from. If I'm careful, I might be able to find my way out of it altogether. But a setback could mean sinking back into it and losing another three years. Can you understand that?"

I'd noticed the small differences in her. The attempts to clean, to dress, to be up. Her appetite and agitation growing. They were subtle, but they were something. She was clawing her way, centimeter by centimeter, out of the pain. I thought of holding Robby's urn in my arms, smelling him all around me, seeing him in the dozens of memories that sprang up with every item my eyes fell on in the storage unit. That experience wouldn't just wound her—it would end her.

I nodded slowly.

She exhaled, and I realized she'd been holding her breath waiting for my answer.

"Mom," I said carefully, seeing my moment. I *had* to try. "If you really want to get better, you know you have to get rid of them—*all* of them."

Her head jerked up. "I'm going to see Dr. Rothchild on Monday. He's adjusting my doses. I will get better, Olivia. It will take time."

I knew Dr. Rothchild. He'd peddle LSD tabs to elementary kids in a clown suit if he thought he could get away with it and make some money. We'd been through the dose adjustments before. They just shuffled her addiction from one set of pills to another, raising and lowering different things in an attempt to look like they were actually doing something, like they cared. It was a game we all played, pretending she had any intention of getting off.

"It's not enough," I said quietly.

"What? What was that?"

My eyes, backed by steel, met hers. "It won't be enough. You know that."

"Olivia, how can you—"

"Because it's not medicine, Mom. Not the way you're using it. And you're not sick. They're drugs. And you're an addict. It's just that no one's had the nerve to say it to your face because they feel sorry for you. But I don't."

Her eyes were glassy, her face slackening with shock. "Olivia!"

"Not anymore. We all lost Robby. Not just you. Not just Dad. I loved him too. And I lost him. I had to find him like that, see the life drained out of him. What do you think that was like? I'll live my whole life knowing that if I had only done one thing differently, my brother might still be alive. Do you live with that? Do you know what it feels like to know your own mother blames you for your brother's death? Don't try to deny it. Have more respect for us both than that."

She shifted in her chair, her mouth opening and then closing again.

"You're an addict. Dad's a nutcase. And I'm a murderer." I rose from the table and started for the stairs, too tired to watch her choke on my words.

"Olivia!" she shouted, jumping up. "Wait."

I paused at the doorway of the kitchen and turned to face her.

Her eyes filled with three years' worth of unshed tears, spilling over and down her yellowed cheeks as she trembled where she stood. "It wasn't your fault, sweetie. I know what I said, and it was wrong. It wasn't your fault. It wasn't."

I pursed my lips and folded my arms, breathing sharply in through my nose before turning for the stairs. "Keep telling yourself that, Mom. Maybe someday we'll all believe it."

On the way to my room, I stopped at hers and swiped a bottle of sleeping pills. I didn't bother to take a few and put it back, turning the label out to cover my tracks. I was sinking into an exhaustion that only a coma could remedy. I took the whole bottle with me to my room. I was done apologizing.

CHAPTER 25

I slept for three days. Mostly. Facing the truth was even more exhausting than running from it. I had believed I was doing the right thing, confronting all the unspoken horrors of our family, or at least it was different, and different felt better. But I was digging into three years of backstocked emotion, and it was wearing me thin. I wanted to turn it all off for a while. I would wake just long enough to use the bathroom and eat something, to drag my laptop out and Google phrases like "family curse" and "death fetishes." I dug up a lot of superstition and BDSM. Nothing that really explained Kara's behavior the other day. I'd grow bored or frustrated, push the laptop away, sink into my pillows, and drift off again. If I couldn't fall right back to sleep, I'd pop another of Mom's pills. She didn't seem to miss them, since she never came inquiring. But she had more than one option for coma in a bottle, and I knew that when I took these.

At one point, I thought I heard my father outside my door

calling my name. His voice sounded stretched, like a deflated balloon over an open glass. I laid there, my eyes fixed on the depressed rectangles of my paneled door, listening to him. But I couldn't bring myself to respond. He went away eventually, and I fell back asleep only to wake later, wondering if it had happened at all.

In my dreams, Robby was trapped in an urn, screaming for me to let him out. I'd try and try to pry the gleaming soapstone halves apart. In most of them, I'd resort to pounding the urn against a cold, concrete floor, to no avail. Eventually, like my father, his cries would weaken and disappear, and I would wake to a pillowcase soaked in tears, which I would just flip over.

In the last dream, I finally managed to shatter the urn, beating it against the concrete slab like an ape trying to crack a coconut. Water poured out across the floor, soaking my bare knees. I sloshed through it like I was digging for a penny in a puddle, all desperation and sisterly love. But there was no Robby, not even his ashes. Just waves and waves of water that kept flowing and flowing until I was slipping underneath, where the shadow man waited.

I woke from this dream to find Kara standing over my bed, the water that slicked her hair dripping across my face, my nest of sheets and duvet. It was 2:00 a.m.

I tried to wipe my eyes and push myself up, but my arms felt strangely weak. I couldn't tell at first if she was another dream, like Robby crying, like my father calling me. But the chill in the water falling off her, the clattering of her jaw, the flashing whites of her too-wide eyes eventually convinced me this was no mirage but the flesh-and-blood version standing over me in the middle of the night.

"You should tell your parents to lock the door," she said flatly.

"Kara? What are you doing here? Why are you all wet?"

Her arms were folded across her chest, but I could see her skin glowing through the oversize white T-shirt that plastered it like a wet Band-Aid. She was drenched head to toe and shoeless.

"You know that gully Prescott took us to?"

I nodded, forcing myself up to find a towel among the scattering of dirty clothes on my floor. When I located one, I wrapped it around her shoulders.

"I followed it."

"Where? Why?"

But Kara wasn't dictated by the why's of life, and she ignored my second question. "There's a tunnel."

"You mean a culvert?"

"Whatever."

"Kara, that's dangerous. Those gullies flood all the time from the rain. You can't just wade through them."

"It was so dark," she whispered. Not in a way that seemed frightened, but in a way that seemed electrified.

I scowled at her. "Right. 'Cause it's two o'clock in the morning and you were standing in a tunnel under the road."

But she didn't seem to register my logic. "It just kept going and going, Olivia. Deeper and deeper and deeper."

Now I began to panic a little. Culverts weren't usually very long or very deep. Where had she been exactly? "Kara, let me walk you home, okay? Before you end up getting sick running around at night soaking wet."

I placed my hands on either side of her shoulders, but she shook me off.

"I'm not a child, Olives. I know what I saw."

I took a steadying breath. "Okay. What did you see?"

"*Him.*"

As soon as the word hissed out of her I felt my skin erupt into goose bumps like a million pinpricks across my body. "Who?"

She pressed her lips together, grinning, a girl sucking on candy secrets. "My father."

I let the impossibility of her statement fold over me, let it shake the last dregs of sleep from my mind.

"Kara, listen to me. That's not possible. I don't know who you saw or what they gave you, but it wasn't your father." I crossed my arms, determined to talk some sense into her.

She chuckled under her breath. "Poor Olivia. You think you know me. You think you know something about my family. Don't you?" She stumbled in place, then regained her footing, glaring at me. "Whatever you think you know, forget it. Truth is always stranger than fiction, right? Isn't that what people say?"

I shrugged. "Whatever, Kara. I think we should just get you home."

She shook her head like an impudent child. "Aren't you listening to me? That house across the street is not my home. Everything is changing, Olivia. Can't you feel it? The world slanting under our feet like a giant Tilt-A-Whirl? He'll call for me soon. He told me so. And once that happens, nothing will be the same."

I felt a fire in my belly ignite. Low and hot, it curdled my thoughts, soured my feelings. I was done playing games. "Come on. I'm walking you home. You're high or something."

But she folded her legs in the middle of my room and refused to budge.

After several long minutes trying to drag her, reason with her, and even bribe her with leftover sleeping pills, I gave up. I dug through my bed until I found my cell phone and dialed Prescott.

I had to call three times before he answered.

"This better be good."

"Meet me out front."

"Now?" He sounded hoarse and more than a little pissed.

"Please. I need your help."

"Okay. Give me a minute."

I left Kara shivering on my floor and went out to get him. He was marching down the sidewalk in a muscle shirt and sweatpants.

"What the hell, Olivia? It's like three a.m."

"I know. I'm sorry. I didn't know who else to call. She won't leave."

"Who?"

"Kara. She turned up in my room soaking wet and making zero sense half an hour ago. I need to get her home but she won't come with me. Something's…something's wrong with her."

Prescott smirked. "Well, we already knew that, didn't we?"

"No, not in the usual way. Come inside and see."

"Won't your parents get upset?"

"We're not exactly on speaking terms right now. They won't know. Just be quiet."

We snuck in through the front and crept up the stairs, the light from my room leaking under the crack of the door at the end of the hall. I opened it and dragged him in quickly, closing it behind me.

Kara took one look at him and jumped up, throwing her arms out and wrapping him in a giant, sloppy, damp hug, but not before he got a load of her wet T-shirt contest attire. "Prescott!"

"Shhh." He peeled her off him, and I handed him the towel she'd thrown off only a moment ago. Wrapping her back in it, he said, "Come on, Kara. Let's get you to bed."

Docile as a sedated kitten, she followed him down the stairs and out front across the street. I stayed a couple of paces behind. When he got her up the steps, I tried the knob, but the door was locked. Sybil must have come in from a smoke without realizing Kara wasn't home and locked it behind her. I pushed the doorbell and waited, praying someone would hear.

A few moments later, the front door opened, and Rhea stood there in an oversize green knit shawl with sleep-tossed hair. "Olivia?"

I pushed Kara toward her. "Sorry, Mrs. Hallas. I found her like this. She was in my room. She won't tell me where she's been, but I'm worried about her."

Kara dropped my towel and scooted around her mother's frame, pirouetting on one toe like a drunk ballerina. "I found it, Mother," she said, laughing. "I found the way!"

Rhea grasped at her, coming up empty-handed. "To where, Kara? The way to where?"

That's when I saw Sybil standing behind them both, her hair a silver-wire halo, gleaming in the half-light. "The way to Hell," she said plainly, her voice creaking like her rocker.

"Okay, I'm gonna go now," I said, backing away. "We just came to drop her off."

Rhea seemed to take in Prescott for the first time, his muscled arms and boyish charm. "Who are you? Were you with my daughter?"

"No, ma'am," he blurted.

"He's a friend," I clarified. "I called him to help. That's all."

I watched the knowing smile crawl across Sybil's face as Rhea shut the door, her milk-glass eyes fixed where Prescott stood.

We walked slowly back to our side of the street, glancing over our shoulders now and again.

"That old woman is creepy," Prescott said with a shudder. "Christ."

"They're all a little *different*."

"That's one way of putting it."

I chuckled at his sarcasm. He was right. *Different* was the understatement of the century. "I won't go back to sleep now."

He watched me, thinking. "Me neither. You got a place to hang in back?"

"Maybe, why? Are we gonna sit out here all night?"

"Just long enough to smoke this," he said, pulling a joint from a pocket in his sweatpants.

I led him behind our garage, where my dad had caught me and Kara only—how many days ago was that now? My summer was beginning to blur. The one good thing about our record-breaking drought was that the usual cloud of mosquitos wasn't hovering. With no rainwater collecting in upturned buckets, birdbaths, or low spots, there were no stagnant pools or puddles for the bloodsuckers to rear their young. I mentally added *no mosquitos* to the list of things I was grateful for. It was a short list.

"I've never smoked weed before," I told him.

Prescott laughed. "You take that shit of your mother's, but you're afraid of a little joint?"

"I didn't say I was afraid. Just inexperienced."

"It's real simple," he said, pausing to get it lit. "Just inhale, dummy."

I slid down into the grass, leaning against the garage, and inhaled until my lungs burned like cigarette paper, coughing violently after.

Prescott took a seat next to me, patting me on the back until I relaxed.

We sat in silence, taking hits in turn, simmering over the weirdness of the night, of the summer.

At last, when my muscles felt like half-boiled noodles and my head was stuffed with fuzzy wool, I turned to Prescott. "Something's going on with Kara."

"You think?"

"It's not just tonight. She's acted weird before this. It's getting worse, like something is building."

He looked beyond the hollows crowning my cheekbones

and the red lightning no doubt spiderwebbing the whites of my eyes. "You're really worried about her."

I nodded.

Prescott took another drag, held steady, and released the smoke in a slow, practiced stream. "Don't be."

"How can you say that? After tonight?"

He faced me. "Olivia, whatever Kara is, she's not like us. And that's what we love about her. Expecting her to act like us, like anyone but her own crazy self, would be senseless. Try to change her, and you destroy everything she is. Let it be."

I thought about telling him about the kiss, but the timing felt all wrong, and his indifference irritated me. "What are you implying?"

"That you have a habit of holding on too tight."

Did he mean with him or just with Kara? "Like when?"

"Like always," he laughed. "You wanted us to stay the same, but we couldn't. You're doing it now," he said quietly. "And not just with me. You've held too tightly to Robby these past three years, and it's dragging you down with him."

I couldn't argue, so I didn't. Instead, I leaned my head back and closed my eyes, feeling the water from my dream flow and flow and flow, until my head slipped under, where *he* was waiting. Always waiting.

CHAPTER 26

I waited until the next afternoon to check on Kara. I cleaned up and found a box of cookies in the kitchen pantry that I dumped into an old holiday tin lined with paper napkins. Then I marched across the street with my meager offering for the ladies of the Hallas household, feeling oddly anxious about seeing Rhca again, as though it were my fault Kara had turned up practically naked and dripping wet in my bedroom during the night.

I noticed Sybil's rocker was empty. She'd been abandoning her post more and more of late. At first, her constant presence there unnerved me, like unwanted video surveillance. But now it felt more comforting, like a trusty watchdog. Not for the first time, I wondered about her age, her health. She looked like she could have been the Crypt Keeper's nanny, but she couldn't be older than eighty-five. Maybe ninety? And yet Rhea still looked so young. The puzzle of their ages did not fit together as a proper puzzle should. It was all angles and edges, no neatly rounded lobes and curves.

I knocked twice on the front door and waited.

Rhea opened it slowly, her long hair braided, her face a little grave. Instantly, I worried Kara had worsened over the night.

My words faltered. "I—I, uh, brought these for you. How's Kara?"

Before her mother could open her mouth, Kara herself appeared over her shoulder. Her hair was dry as kindling and bright as polished brass. Her cheeks blushed in all the right places. Her lips were full and dark as ripe strawberries. Everything about her was somehow…*more*.

"Kara?"

She ducked around her mother and grabbed me by the arm, pulling me out onto the porch. "I've got this, Mom," she insisted. And then, "I'm fine. Really," when Rhea hesitated before closing the door on us.

"How are you?" I began, a barrage of questions beginning to hammer away in my brain, desperate for release.

"I'm fine," she said with a look that was half-puzzled and half-irritated.

"But last night…you were—"

"Forget last night. I need to talk to you. You aren't going to believe this." Her manner was fevered and almost manic, giddy, but clear as a bell compared to the space cadet I'd met the night before.

"What?"

She whipped an envelope out from inside her waistband. "This! This is it! And I have you to thank. Oh, I almost can't believe it."

"What? Another letter?"

She laughed at my ignorance. "Not *just* a letter, silly, silly Olives. An invitation."

My eyebrows arched of their own volition. "To where?"

"Remember the letter you found me writing the other night? The one to the guy who kind of, well, you know, eats some of his victims?"

"The cannibal? Yeah. I remember. I remember telling you not to write that one anymore."

She beamed, sloughing off my rebuke. "He wants to meet me! Us. He wants to meet *us*."

I frowned at the innocuous paper rectangle. "How? He's in prison." I enunciated each syllable to drive home my point.

"Well, not him exactly. But someone he knows. Like a…a…"

"An envoy?"

"Yeah! Like that."

I stared at her. I was right. She had worsened overnight. "Um. No."

Her face fell, the ecstatic aura around her dimming ever so little. "What do you mean *no*?"

"Kara, anyone this guy knows well enough to do his bidding is dangerous. Hell no."

"Olivia, I don't think you understand. This is huge. This guy, the envoy, he's going to bring us something, something big, in exchange for taking a quick video, a live feed, so Archibald—that's his name—can see us as we are in real time."

"More like in exchange for a pint of blood. Kara, you can't be serious about this. Is this all just some creepy game to you?

Because it's not a game to them. I get that you're a fangirl for the dead, but shit like this, meeting people in person, is the kind of thing that gets your face on the front page of the news, milk-carton style, when they find your body floating in a ravine somewhere."

She took a step forward, her eyes softening at the corners. "Olivia, please. What you and I share, it's more than just a friendship. I think you know that." Her cheeks blushed ever so slightly, as if on cue. "And it's more than what you could have with someone like Prescott. He could never understand *that* part of you. Not like I can."

"What part?" I pretended that her words weren't spiraling into the core of me and nesting there.

"The part that is touched by what we see—have *seen*—that others are too terrified to even glance at. We stare into the void, you and I, without flinching. What I mean is, I've never met someone like you, like *me*, before. Only you can help me do this, Olivia. I want you there, with me, for this."

She spoke as if she were asking me to attend her recital. And in some weird way, maybe that's what this was—a key performance, a coming of age. But this wasn't a test of her piano skills or dance moves, and I latched on to the fear wriggling through me like nightcrawlers under the soil. "I'm not like you, Kara."

Her eyes narrowed, and the unforgiving sun, which had been painting glaring stripes of light across her porch only a moment before, ducked behind a lone cloud, casting all in shadow. "You promised me."

"What?"

She inched toward me until her face was so close to mine I thought she was going to kiss me again. But instead, she whispered, "You. Promised. Me. You can't back out now."

"I never promised you *this*."

"In your mother's house, you swore you'd be there for me when I needed you. Remember?"

In response, I felt the pressure of her fingers on my arms that day flare to life beneath my skin like resurrected bruises. "Yeah, for something legitimate. This is not a need. This is a suicide mission. I care about you, and I'm telling you not to do this."

She glared at me. "You can't stop me."

I doubted I could, but I could try. "I'll tell Rhea."

"Go ahead." She dared me with a mocking chuckle. "You think she doesn't know? You think *she* can stop me? I told you, this is hereditary. Who do you think made me this way?"

I paused at that, suddenly unnerved at the thought of bright and happy Rhea death-obsessed like her daughter. "Kara, don't. Please. This is a terrible idea."

"If you're not going to help me, then stay out of my way," she warned, her gray-blue eyes flaring like neon tubing ran beneath them. "I can tell your parents about the drugs, about us, about everything. I can take Prescott from you, turn everyone against you. You know I can."

My heart stung with the slap of her words. It wasn't whether she could or couldn't manage those things that turned me. It was the betrayal implicit in the threats, whether she achieved them or not. It was the realization that I'd ceased to be a person in the eyes of someone I loved and was nothing more than an instrument to be manipulated.

"Fine. Self-destruct if you want to, but do it on your own." I backed away preparing to leave, anything to get out of her orbit, a pull strong enough to drown in, a maelstrom of Kara.

"Olives, wait!" Her voice shifted into that of a little girl, and she reached for me a moment too late to touch me. "This is for us. We're the Resurrection Girls. I can't do this without you."

I saw my grandmother's ring hanging against a thin finger on her outstretched hand, the stone more gray than I recalled, as though it were troubled. I shook my head and held out the tin of cookies I'd been holding all this time. "Here, I brought these for you."

"Olivia," she all but growled.

"I'm not this, Kara. I'm not. I never was. Not like you. I don't want to die."

"You could have fooled me. Locked away in that coffin of a house, dead as your brother these last three years. Until *I* came for you." She was vacillating between pleading and threatening, her voice barbed with malice one moment and brushed with need the next.

I shook my head, taking another step back. "Not anymore. I'm just sorry that's all I was to you."

"Olivia, please," she pleaded, her eyes beginning to water. "Just come with me."

"I can't." I set the cookies down on the bottom step and turned, bolting for the street, for the old, thirsty oak and the crunchy lawn on the other side, for the distance that would keep me alive.

CHAPTER 27

I wrestled with her words for the next seven hours. I could go back over and apologize, agree to her crazy plan. She'd take me back. She wanted me with her. It was doubtful anyone would actually be there to meet her anyway. Right? Probably it was just some bored convict playing games with her. Didn't they do stuff like that? We'd go and find it was all a ruse, and then we'd get Prescott and smoke a joint after and laugh until our ribs cracked over the stupidity of it all.

And maybe later, after I walked her home, she would kiss me good night and her lips would taste like peppermints and Mary Jane.

Or, in an alternate fantasy, Kara would leave early, and Prescott and I would lie on our backs under the bridge at the gully, still laughing, until our eyes ran with tears. And then he'd lean over me like he did in his room and place his mouth over mine, sucking my breath with warmth and urgency.

Between fantasies, clarity would set in like rigor mortis,

paralyzing my brain in a pattern of fear. My best friend was going to die. She was going to meet some underground, girl-eating, ex-con groupie who would take video all right, video of himself as he squeezed the life out of her and mutilated her body. And I would have to live with the guilt and responsibility of the deaths of two people I cared about in this lifetime, not just one.

I squeezed my eyelids together, trying to force away the images of her lifeless body lying in an abandoned parking lot or buried under a layer of compost along the forest floor. I took two low-dose Xanax from a stash I'd hidden in my pencil box and forgotten about. But nothing was strong enough to wash the fear and urgency away.

I imagined Robby telling me the morning of his death what would happen if I stepped out that door. If I'd known, would I have acted differently?

Of course.

Wasn't this the same thing? I had a chance to make a difference this time. If I didn't take it, I would never forgive myself.

At 8:00 p.m., I picked up my phone and called Prescott.

He answered after one ring. "What's up, Olives?"

"You have to help me." My voice broke, and I suddenly began to tremble all over, as though we had only moments to save her, maybe even were already too late.

"Olivia, what's wrong? You sound upset."

"It's Kara. She's gone too far this time. Or she's about to."

"What do you mean?"

"I went to see her this morning. She told me about this guy, a killer she'd been writing."

"Not this again." He sighed. "I told you two to cut that out."

"Listen to me! I wasn't in on this one, but she acted like I was. She told him we would meet him somewhere. Well, not him, but some friend of his."

"Shit."

"I refused. I told her it was crazy and stupid and a death trap, and she got mad at me. I don't know what to do, Prescott. She won't listen to me, but if she goes and something happens to her…"

I pressed the backs of my fingers to my lips until I could feel my teeth cutting into my knuckles through them. "I can't go through this again. Please. You have to help."

"Olivia, calm down." His voice softened in reflex to my distress. "You did the right thing. Okay? But what can I do? Kara makes her own choices."

I curled in on myself, sucking in air. "You can talk to her. You can try. Please, Prescott. I think something really bad is going to happen if she goes."

I could hear him take in a heavy, resigned breath through the phone. "I'll go knock on her door and try to talk to her, okay? But you have to promise me you are going to calm down. I'm coming to check on you after."

"Yes, okay. I promise." I deliberately tried to slow my breathing, tried to command my voice, tried to halt the tears. I told myself I was in charge of these things, though I didn't believe it.

"Wait for me," he said before hanging up.

I did.

I waited over an hour for him. I checked my phone over and

over again, and when it continually showed he hadn't called, I would go to the window and stare, trying to imagine what was happening in the house across the street.

I looked for Sybil's red cigar eye, but the porch was black and empty.

I worried that Prescott had lied to me. That he hadn't gone to talk to her at all. That he was in his bedroom right now watching sports replays online and laughing at my hysteria.

I worried that I was too late. That he went to her door only to find she was already out, already in the clutches of some cannibal pervert, already dead.

This is stupid, I told myself. *Just go over there and face her.*

The waiting was making me more anxious. When images of Robby's body on the bottom of our pool began to play behind my eyes, I couldn't take another minute. I slipped on my tennis shoes and ran out the front door.

Sybil's rocker was moving slowly back and forth when I crossed the street, as if she had just abandoned it, but the old woman was nowhere to be seen. I knocked and knocked at the Hallases' front door but no one answered. After a few moments, I tried the knob. The door was open, and I pushed inward, calling, "Hello?" as I entered, so as not to alarm anyone.

The kitchen light was out. A soft lamp glowed in Sybil's smoking room to my left, but there was no sign of anyone.

"Rhea? Kara?" I heard a creak in the ceiling above, near Kara's room, and made for the stairs. Maybe her mother and grandmother stepped out for some groceries or something. I would just be a minute anyway. I just needed to be sure Prescott had been here, that he'd talked sense into her. I needed to see her and know she was alive and would stay that way.

The flight of stairs seemed to grow longer with every step. Panic was creeping up the back of my legs. I began taking the stairs two at a time, racing for the top. When my feet met the landing, I paused to breathe and regain my composure. I didn't want her to see me this stricken. Or maybe it was a good thing. Maybe then she'd realize how foolish her plan was.

I neared her door slowly, stretching out my inhales, my exhales, to steady my heart rate. Muffled sounds played out behind the wood, too subtle for me to decipher, but the door was barely cracked. I leaned in to listen and heard a throaty groan escape the room. It was Kara. I was sure of it.

Suddenly the empty house, the open door, made terrible, life-threatening sense. She'd given him her own address. He'd come here and already done something to the older women. Now he was in Kara's room, slowly choking the life out of her. I could only hope Prescott really was in his room across the street watching sports replays. That he wasn't just another victim.

I flung the door wide preparing myself to scream, to pounce, to run, to do something, anything that would detract her attacker. If I could buy her a moment, maybe we'd both survive this somehow.

But the scene unfurling before me was a shock I hadn't prepared myself for. The air ejected from my lungs in a reverse gasp.

They were on her bed, twisted in a knot of arms and legs. Prescott was wedged beneath her, his face craning up to meet hers. Kara straddled him with strong legs, her hair tossed to one side. His shirt was on the floor at my feet. His jeans clearly undone and pushed down. She was still wearing a white lace bra, one strap dangling off her shoulder. I spun around before I could see if her panties were on or off.

I heard them react more than saw it—gasping followed by Prescott cursing. The moan of her mattress, the rustle of sheets as they tried to slide apart, find clothes, gather themselves. But I was already bounding down the stairs and racing for the door. I could hear Prescott calling my name. I could hear his heavy footfalls as he ran down the stairs after me, but I didn't dare stop. I tore across their porch and lawn and hit the pavement of the street without looking, only realizing the car was bearing down on me when the headlights filled my vision.

The shriek of tested brakes screamed between us. I made it to my yard without impact, and the car forced Prescott to stop at the curb. It bought me the extra few seconds I needed to scramble through the front door and lock it behind me.

My mother sat in the living room in front of the television, a pot of water on the stove just beginning to boil. She turned when she heard me slam the door. "Olivia, I'm making pasta. Want to watch some shows with me while it cooks?"

No, no, no. I couldn't do this now, this belated attempt at bonding. "I can't. My, uh, room's a mess and I don't feel well."

I breezed through the kitchen to avoid her. "Tell Prescott I don't want to see him if he knocks."

She stood, watching me make for the stairs. "Olivia, what's going on?"

"I told you. I don't feel good. I think I'm getting sick. I'm just going to take a shower and lie down for a bit."

"Okay." She hesitated. "Call if you need anything."

"Sure."

As I reached the top step, I heard the knock at the front door. She would tell him I wasn't well and he'd leave. He wouldn't press my mom. No one pressed the mother of a dead child.

It wasn't all a lie. My stomach *was* turning somersaults at the memory of them wound around each other. I ducked into my dad's room first, since he clearly wasn't home, and found the bottle of bourbon he liked to hide in his nightstand. I tried not to think of where he was, curled up on Robby's old bed in a storage room a few blocks away. Or maybe tonight just at a bar with some coworkers, overextending their happy-hour ritual. That's what normal dads did when they stayed out late, right?

I took the bottle to my room and locked the door behind me, digging out the pencil case with the old Xanax stash. I took one more pill, ground it between my molars, and washed the powder down with a swig of hellfire, wondering what possessed anyone to drink bourbon if they had a choice.

If I could just sleep long and deep enough, I might stop seeing Kara draped over him.

CHAPTER 28

In my mind, the ambulance was bearing down a bustling Houston street as it screamed its way toward the medical center with Robby, lifeless, in the back. The siren wailed so loud my ears rang with its echoes, and yet my baby brother's silence was louder still. No breaths. No giggles. No cries.

I could see the EMT hunched over him, hands folded in defeat. I could smell the antiseptic that characterized all medical establishments, moving or otherwise. I could just barely make out his blond hair through lights so bright they washed all in a haze of white. *Duck hair*, we'd called it. Fuzzy and sticking straight up, like he had a permanent case of static electricity.

These bright-as-day flashes were pockmarked with frequent blackouts, periods of brooding dark where the only thing I was aware of was a sickening sense of unrest. A need to move without the limbs to do so. A craving for air without the lungs to take it in. A desire for substance—action—in a world of vacant inertia.

And the boy on the gurney was so pale he disappeared, simply fading into the starched white sheet beneath him. And then he wasn't a boy at all, but a girl with flat, dark hair, straight eyebrows, and a very weak pulse.

I know that girl came the dull but persistent revelation, piercing my brain like an ice pick with the steady thrum of a mallet behind it. *Chip, chip, chip.*

I *was* that girl.

Such were my memories of my overdose. If you can call them memories at all.

I didn't see a white light or hear angels singing. I didn't sit at the feet of God or wander through heavenly meadows populated by ancestors I had never known in waking life but was fond of nonetheless. I didn't actually die, so maybe that's why all I could recall after regaining consciousness twenty-seven hours later were the blurred and dreamlike alternating visions of myself and my brother riding in the back of an ambulance.

They pumped my stomach and then gave me some kind of anti-Xanax drug that caused me to have a seizure before my vitals began to stabilize, and they held me a couple of days more to be sure there'd be no more seizures. Or at least that's what the doctor told me right before signing the papers for my release.

"You're a very lucky young woman," he said in a tone that actually said, *You're a very stupid young woman and they don't pay me enough for this.*

His eyes met my mother's across the hospital bed. "She'll need plenty of rest and hydration. And she'll have to be watched for a while." That time, his tone sounded more like *Think you can dry out long enough to hide your pills from your daughter?*

My mother nodded. The rims of her eyes and tip of her nose were the color of Pepto-Bismol and just as runny. It looked like someone had been stuffing cotton beneath her lids, they were so puffy. "Of course," she said obediently, using her professional voice. A voice I hadn't heard her use in a long, long time.

I twisted the little plastic band around my wrist, feeling uncomfortable that I was being discussed in the third person.

"You said your husband was coming to pick you up?" His expression was skeptical.

"He was," she began, "but something came up. I'll drive her home."

The doctor reluctantly passed her the paperwork. "Take these. Read them. There is a list of nearby treatment facilities in there, as well as necessary hotline numbers and support groups. Your daughter will need help, Mrs. Foster, if she's going to kick this habit."

She nodded solemnly.

Habit? Since when did I become the one with the habit? This was her habit, not mine. And yet something told me arguing that point here and now would leave me looking more guilty, not less. Desperation and quicksand—better not to struggle or you'll only sink deeper.

A fog of irony cushioned the spaces between me, my mother, and the doctor.

"A social worker will be in touch." With that, he *whooshed* out of the room, his white lab coat trailing like Jedi cosplay.

"A social worker?" I looked to my mother. "What does that mean?"

She inhaled sharply through her nose. "We'll talk about it on the way. Right now, let's just get you home. Okay?"

They insisted on wheeling me to the car, like somehow Xanax plus bourbon equaled double amputation.

When the doors were safely closed and securely locked, and the parking lot was fading in the rearview, I turned to my mother. "Are you okay to do this? Drive, I mean?"

She nodded stiffly. "I'm clear. I can drive."

But the truth was, she'd hardly left the house since Robby's death. And the pills made safety questionable behind the wheel.

"Mom, it's okay." I put a hand out and brushed her forearm. "You can pull over up ahead. I'll drive us home."

Her eyes met mine, and the terror and agony filling them was enough to swallow a hundred summers in a hundred years. She didn't speak, but she wept, truly *wept*, as she turned into the gas station, utterly defeated. And sitting in the parking lot of a rundown Shell station with three working pumps and a broken dumpster overflowing with urban detritus, the engine humming between us, the plastic hospital band flopping in slow circles around my wrist, I finally saw my mother for what she was. Not just a broken woman, but a shell. If she was ever going to be right again, she'd have to rebuild from scratch because losing Robby had left her with nothing. She could never be that woman I remembered, and there was no point hating her for it. But maybe she could become someone we could both live with.

Before we traded places, she looked at me, wrapping my face in her palms. "I wanted to be strong for you." Her bottom lip quivered and her chin puckered in this way that broke my heart. Tears streamed down, catching in her lips. "But I realize something now. Something it's taken me three years and two lost children to understand. I cannot do this alone."

She crumpled into me, and I wrapped my arms protectively around her as we both cried.

"I love you so much, Olivia. I can't lose you too. And I almost did."

We sat up after several minutes, untangling our arms and wiping our faces. "You come drive for me," she said quietly. "But I promise you, this will be the last time. I don't need the doctor's list; I've been doing my own research."

A hint of a smile played at the corners of her mouth, though smiling still seemed unfamiliar to her. "I'm checking in to a facility next week. I've already given them a deposit and told your father."

"Next week?" I tried to swallow the nearness of it. Isn't this what I wanted? My mother back—her recovery, her wellness? And yet I'd never considered it would mean her leaving.

"I want to be sure you're okay before I go." She patted my leg, then folded her hands in her lap, looking away from me. "I'm not the only one who needs support, Olivia."

"What do you mean?"

"The hospital has assigned you a caseworker. You're a minor who overdosed on a prescription that wasn't yours." She braved a glance at my face. "Generally, that's seen as a welfare issue."

"Do I have to go away? Like you?"

She shook her head. "No. But you'll need counseling from a professional who specializes in substance abuse in adolescents. We have to show that you are actively working on recovery, not using...*anything*."

I glanced guiltily out the window, where a homeless man was trying to clean the windshield of a nearby car in hopes of a handout.

"Your blood alcohol level was very high, Olivia. And they found marijuana as well as the sedatives in your system."

I cringed, remembering my evening behind the garage with Prescott, remembering Prescott at all.

"I'm not like you," I murmured, more to myself than her. "I was upset, that's all."

"Olivia." She waited until I turned to face her. "We're all upset, and we have every reason to be. But we have to do better. Do you understand? Or what we have left of this family will be taken from us too."

I nodded.

"Come on. Your turn."

I crawled out of the car and walked around, climbing in and buckling into the driver's seat. "Your treatment, it feels so sudden."

"I know," she said whisper soft. "But it's not. It's taken three years and one hell of a scare to get here."

CHAPTER 29

We were a solid twelve blocks away from the turn into our neighborhood when we first saw the flames.

They licked along a dry, abandoned field to our left, one of those lots that has been waiting, overlooked in the shadow of progress, for a decade to be adopted by the right developers and turned into a strip mall or office park. Their tongues were low and yellow orange, the color of construction barrels, and running in parallel lines, like tiger stripes in the dead grass.

It was so out of place along a busy road that we didn't even have the good sense to be scared, just kind of surprised, like when you see a coyote next to the highway and you remember, if only for a moment, that nature has not been entirely vanquished. But as the cars in front of us began to slow down over the next few blocks and the shrill sirens of gathered fire engines ripped the Band-Aid off my prehospital, ambulatory memories, it dawned that something was very, very wrong.

Eventually, we found ourselves at a dead standstill in the

far-right lane in the middle of Westpoint Village Road. We had the good fortune to be stopped just shy of a corner store's driveway and, with a little honking, persuaded the car in front of us to scoot up so we could pull in and park. We both got out and made our way toward the ditch separating the crowded parking lot from the congested snake of vehicles.

"What's happening?" my mom asked the potbellied man standing next to her with a Big Gulp in one hand.

"Fire," he stated as if it were obvious. And that much was.

Then he turned to look at us, his eyes falling questionably on the plastic band around my wrist. Too late, I tucked my fists into my armpits.

"They're breaking out all over the city," he offered in a gentler tone. "They've got trucks turned on it up ahead, where it's at its worst. Trying to keep it contained until it burns itself out. As long as it doesn't jump the street, it should settle down soon enough. But there's a few things in its path that are worrisome. Two snow cone stands and a storage facility have already caught."

My mother nodded along until he got to the end. Her brow furrowed. "Did you say a storage facility?"

"Yeah, up ahead a few blocks. It's too late for that place. Idiots put a shingle roof on it—that caught first. It's burning from the inside out, but they think they can keep it inside the parking lot there. Spare the neighborhoods. That's the real concern. Damn drought."

She turned to me, her eyes blooming into blisters of white-hot fear.

"Dad," I said, catching on.

"He was going to clean something out. He said he wanted us to start over. That's why he didn't come to drive you home. I tried asking him to wait, but he was so insistent."

I grabbed her hand and pulled her behind me into the street, running between rows of cars and trucks whose engines had been turned off in resignation to the situation at hand. We tore down three blocks worth of asphalt before we hit a barricade of fire trucks, ambulances, squad cars, and orange emergency cones.

I ducked between two cones with her at my heels, running full-tilt toward what I could see was row upon row of blue-doored storage units blazing before us—though I mostly saw reams of ash-laden smoke and the orange lick of fire reaching toward a cloudless Houston sky. We were nearly to the parking lot when a man grabbed my arm, whipping me around and stopping us short.

"Hey, hey! You need to get back. You aren't allowed past that point," he said, throwing a finger in the direction we'd just come.

His pressed blue shirt and badge dinged *cop* like an alarm bell through my mind. "My dad's in there," I shouted back. "Please, you have to let us pass."

My mom quickly pulled me from his grasp, pushing her body in front of mine. "Oh thank goodness, Officer. My husband is in that facility. Can you help us?"

His face contorted as though he wasn't sure whether to believe us or not. "Ma'am, everyone has been evacuated from the premises. If your husband was inside the building, he's not now."

"Evacuated?"

In a desperate ploy for sympathy, I threw my hospital-braceleted arm up around my mother's shoulders so that the officer couldn't miss the tag. It's not like it said I put myself there. For all he knew, I was seriously ill.

His eyes puckered, etching a spray of deep lines on either end. "They're treating a few people for smoke inhalation over this way. I'll walk you over to look for your husband."

He guided us to the back of an open ambulance, where paramedics were placing shiny plastic masks over the noses of a handful of people. It took a second before I saw him. He was sitting curbside, his dress shirt rolled up to his elbows and his head dropped into his hands.

"Dad!" I yelled. "Dad!"

He looked up, saw us, and started to rise.

My mother reached him first, wrapping an arm around his side for support.

His face looked streaked with dirt. And then I saw that in fact the streaks were clean tracks where tears had swept away a film of smoke and ash.

"I tried," he croaked out. "I tried to save him."

"Shhh." My mother tried to coax him. "Enough, Richard. Sit down." She pushed him back down to the pavement, where we squatted near him.

"Everything was filling with smoke. It happened so fast. I tried to go back in for the urn, but they wouldn't let me. He's lost to us now. Lost to us."

"Shhh," she repeated. "You're okay. That's what matters. We're all okay."

After a while, his shoulders relaxed, his sobs melting into hiccups and then a slow, steady breathing that indicated he was spent. We stood for another hour watching unit 219 burn. Our arms were roped around one another as we watched our memories of my brother melt, watched his ashes scatter among the ashes of old photo albums and used mattresses and clothes people would never wear again. It was the only burial we were going to get. Three years late, but right on time.

Standing in front of that runaway fire—in the worst drought on record, in the most unforgettable summer of my life, fresh out of the hospital from an overdose, heartbroken seven different ways, with my drug-addicted mother and emotionally shattered father—I realized what I think my brother would have wanted me to know all along.

Nothing could take Robby from us. Not a pool. Not a fire. Not a man made of shadows bearing the kiss of death. My brother's body, his duck hair and pudgy arms, his gummy smile and baby-boy smell—those were gone. And they would be missed and longed for every day that we drew breath. But the essence of Robby—his gentle ways, his joy, his truth—would always be ours. He would remain three years bright as dawn, starlit and flawless, a golden promise that finally came and went in perfect tempo.

CHAPTER 30

It was evening before we were finally allowed to pass into our neighborhood, before the flames were satisfactorily extinguished and the immediate danger passed. We pulled into an empty drive, our white house squatting like a ghost on the dead lawn. Even here, the smoke stung my nostrils as I got out of the car. The blinds had been left open, our windows bare to the world. And I was struck by my home as if I'd been away for a very long time and just returned. For all its vacancy, it was still filled with light.

I couldn't deny myself a glance across the street. To my surprise, Sybil sat in her customary rocker, her cigar burning like a flare in the wilting shadows of a late dusk. But when she saw me looking at her, she rose, stubbed out her stogie, and went inside without a gesture.

I turned away, feeling the burn of betrayal light me up inside as we'd watched the wildfires eat at the husks of vegetation bordering the streets. Did she know what I'd witnessed?

Did she see my hospital bracelet, cloudy like her eyes? Did she smell the drugs in me, the purge?

I followed my parents into the house, wondering.

My mother instantly put on the news, she and my dad sitting back on the sofa in a fit of normalcy. As the man with the Big Gulp claimed, ours was not the only fire in Houston. Flames had erupted around the city, in dry lots and empty buildings, as though an army of phantom arsonists had passed through town. The fire department was managing well enough, came the reassuring report from the level-headed, brunette anchor. Most of the sites had been small, uneventful. It was the simultaneous nature of the events that was truly inexplicable, though all pointed to the drought as the culprit. Smokers were lambasted for reckless cigarette tossing.

"I'm going upstairs," I said to the backs of their heads. "I just want to clean some things up."

"Keep your door open," my father insisted.

"We'll be here," my mother added.

I snatched a trash bag from the kitchen on my way.

My room was exactly as I'd left it. I looked for signs of what had happened to me—overturned items where I'd fallen, dried crusts of drool or vomit, something that said, *Olivia was here*—but there were none.

Except the missing doorknob.

My mom had explained in the hospital that when I hadn't answered her knocking, they'd removed it to get in, finding me out cold on the floor. I ran my index finger around the rough wood inside the hole, wondering how my father had expected me to close it. I decided not to ask for it back. I was learning to be at ease with holes in my life.

It only took a short sweep to clean it out. I opened drawers and dug through clothes, finding small stashes here and there, places where I'd tucked "a few" away for later. My mother's pills were easy enough to get directly from the source. I hadn't required much stock of my own. I even found a couple of empty prescription bottles. All went into the trash bag. On a roll, I continued with the normal things. Piling dirty clothes into the forgotten hamper in the corner. Emptying the small wicker trash can under my desk. Straightening the bed and pillows. I got the vacuum from the hall closet and made tracks in the carpet. I found a wash rag and wiped off my desk and shelves, erasing a year's worth of dust.

Then I sat on the edge of my bed holding a plastic bag full of regret, feeling the Hallases' home burning a hole in my back through the window. I would have to face her eventually, face them both. But not today. My phone was dead, had run out of battery during my hospital stay. I left it next to the charger cord, taking solace in the black screen. I had been disconnected for so long. What would another few nights matter?

I was halfway to the garage to dump my bag when the sound of knocking at the front door nearly sent me out of my skin. My mother placed a hand on my father's shoulder, collected herself, and answered it. I stood behind her right shoulder, taking in the orange of Rhea's hair in our front porch light.

"Is Olivia here?"

My mother turned to me, mouth open.

I stepped forward.

Rhea's normally placid face was stricken, muscles knotted beneath the skin, lips thin, color blanched. Her hair needed a fresh combing, and a gray shawl was wrapped tightly around her shoulders as though it was holding her together. Her eyes glistened with damp. "Olivia, thank goodness. I need to ask you something, and I need you to be very, very honest with me. Okay?"

I nodded, sending my mother a glance designed to let her know I had no idea what this was about. She moved to one side but hovered protectively near. "Okay."

Rhea sniffed. "Is Kara here?"

I shook my head. "No. Why?"

Rhea wrung her hands, pulling her shawl tighter. "Please, Olivia. It's okay if she is. You're not in any trouble. I just need to know where my daughter is."

"I promise you, Mrs. Hallas, Kara isn't here." As proof, I held up my left wrist. "I've been in the hospital. See?"

She nodded hesitantly as though this evidence wasn't exactly as solid as I thought it was. "Have you spoken to her? Texted, maybe? Did she tell you where she was going?"

I shook my head. "No, I haven't."

"You're certain?"

My mother stepped closer. "Mrs. Hallas, my daughter wasn't in any condition to speak with anyone the last few days. I can assure you of that. She's had no visitors other than her father and I."

Rhea huddled beneath her shawl, worried. She seemed to register the undeniable truth of it but still resist whatever it meant. "I see."

"Olivia will reach out if she hears anything from your daughter, but right now, she needs to rest."

Rhea ducked her head, started to turn away.

"How long has Kara been gone?"

This once-vibrant woman looked at me, and I could suddenly see her mother's likeness, Sybil, etched in her own features. "Three days."

The air in my lungs dried up. "The police?"

She shook her head. "A girl Kara's age is just a runaway to them. They're not interested in locating her, say she'll come home when she's good and ready."

I recalled her standing in the dark of my room, her wet hair dripping over me as she spoke of things that couldn't be, made no sense. I felt her reaching out to me from the porch steps, begging me to go with her. My stomach clenched on the fear curdling within it. I had been wrong before. I thought she'd brought her pen pal home, that she was in jeopardy, when all she was up to was getting revenge for my rejection. But I knew I wasn't wrong now. "Check her room."

"Pardon?"

"Kara was planning to meet someone, someone who'd written her. Look for his letters and maybe you can figure out where she went. Give those to the police. Maybe then they'll believe you."

Rhea backed away. "Yes, I will. Thank you, Olivia. And if you hear anything?"

"I'll come right to you," I promised.

I ran upstairs after closing the door and plugged my phone in, checking every couple of minutes until it finally had enough juice to come on. I waited hopefully for everything to load, praying she'd tried one last time to convince me, to reach me. That there'd be a message or at the very least her number in the call log.

But she hadn't tried to call. No voice mails either. And no messages.

CHAPTER 31

Kara was staying silent, wherever she was, but Prescott messaged me seven times in all. I read his texts over and over until I fell asleep with the phone in my hand.

Olivia, I'm so sorry.

Please reply.

It didn't mean anything. We're still friends, right?

I know you're angry. I wasn't thinking.

Are you there? Olives?

I'm such an ass. Please forgive me.

It just happened. You know how she is.

Yes, I did. And I'd tried to forget with the help of sedatives and bourbon. But even the burn of my father's hidden booze and my mother's pills couldn't wipe her from my memory. The feel of her skin. The wink of the skull at her neck. The sound of her begging me to go with her.

She was there in my dreams, crossing a river that wound like a black thread through the belly of the world, naked on her knees, poling a raft made of bones. I reached out to her from the bank, my feet sinking into deep mud, afraid to step into the water. And she hovered just beyond my fingertips, laughing at me.

I woke with her laughter ringing in my ears.

And then the pounding drowned it out.

I threw my blankets off and rushed downstairs, hearing the creak of the front door just as my bare feet hit the cold of our kitchen tile. My mother was already there, her robe tied at the waist, her hair pushed back from her face. Rhea filled the doorway, hair wild like the fires that consumed the broken and unhappy corners of our city earlier that day. She leaned in, frantically trying to explain something as my mother pulled away from her.

I rushed up. "What's going on? Did you find her?"

"Yes, that's what I've been trying to say, you must come. Now." She tugged at my shirtfront. "Please, I need your help. Both of you. We can't waste any more time."

My mother's face was ashen, uncertain. She knew nothing of these women who had dominated my summer like the drought itself, unleashing themselves on an unsuspecting world. I wrapped a hand in hers. "Mom, come on. Let's go."

"I don't think that's wise. This is really none of our concern."

Rhea wheeled on us. "Olivia, please?"

"She's my friend," I told my mother. "Stay or come with me."

She pursed her lips but followed, a step behind, as we waded into the night.

Rhea's bedroom was lit by two small lamps and a ceiling fan with only one working bulb. They cast shadows across the walls that looked like dancing phantoms. Sybil huddled near the side of a king-size bed, where Kara was propped on a stack of pillows, her face sweaty at the hairline, eyes squeezed shut. The old woman popped a chip of ice cube in Kara's mouth from a plastic cup and wiped at her forehead with a light cloth.

I looked up at the rafters overhead, feeling the ghost of the hanged man there, his desperation palpable in this room.

Rhea moved toward the bed. "How is she?"

"Stable," the old woman croaked. "For now."

Rhea turned to me and gestured. "Come, Olivia. Kara needs you."

I inched closer, afraid to let my eyes settle anywhere. Kara was there before me, but something wasn't right. And yet the fog of my mind stubbornly refused to part long enough for me to understand it. It wasn't until I was looming over the foot of the bed, my shadow falling long over her form like an omen, that I saw what didn't fit.

Kara's stomach bulged like ripe fruit under her gown, large as a perigee moon and just as round. Her legs were splayed out beneath it like sticks in a snowman. Her face contorted in pain, and she grit her teeth, clenching out a slow wail as a contraction seized her.

"They come fast now," Sybil whispered. "It will be soon."

Rhea nodded.

"Olivia!" Kara gasped, opening her eyes as the contraction was passing.

"I'm here." I moved closer, bending down to let her squeeze my hand. Behind me, my mother gasped as she registered Kara's condition.

Kara wrapped both hands around mine, squeezing as though to reassure herself I was truly there. My grandmother's aquamarine ring was gone, and her hands seemed smaller without it. Why hadn't I ever noticed how fine her bones were?

She pulled me down to her, and I leaned in as far as I could, her pregnant belly keeping me from getting any closer.

"You were right," she whispered in my ear. Before she could say anything else, another labor pain gripped her, and I felt the smooth muscles of her stomach go rigid beneath me.

"Shhh. Don't worry about that now. Just be still."

Kara whimpered, and the audacity that had been her calling card seemed a thousand miles away in this close room. "No, you were right. I'm glad you didn't come with me."

Another contraction followed by another low wail. I squeezed Kara's hand even tighter, shaking my head. "I should have been there to protect you." Though I still wasn't sure from what. I'd been convinced Kara was running toward her own end, and yet she'd returned ripe with a new beginning. What exactly happened over the last three days might never be explained.

Kara's fine hair at her temples was plastered to the sides of her face. "No, Olives," she panted. "You could never save me. Don't you see that by now? This was always my road. I never had a choice. But you made yours, and I'm happy you did."

I gripped her through another contraction, smoothing the hair back from her face. My mind couldn't make heads or tails of what she was saying, and yet my heart understood perfectly. I gave her a small nod.

"You should know," she began, only to be interrupted by another forceful pain. "You should know that Prescott and I—we never—"

I pushed the image of them together out of my head. "Don't, Kara. You don't have to."

"Yes, I do. I want you to know the truth. You walked in before anything could happen."

I wasn't sure I believed her, and yet I desperately wanted to. When three people love each other, no one wins. "Kara, you're telling me this baby, it's not *his*."

She shook her head. "No, that would be impossible."

I stared at her, disbelieving. "It's impossible anyway. How are you…?"

Her eyes latched on to mine, and the depth of sadness within them could have swallowed me. She reached a hand up to brush my face. "I tried to tell you."

I searched my brain for what, in any number of crazy things Kara had said in the time I'd known her, could explain what I was witnessing now. "The curse."

She smiled weakly at me. "That's my Olives."

My mother approached Rhea. "I can call an ambulance."

"No!" Sybil got to her feet, rounding on her.

Rhea put a hand out to still her mother. "Thank you, but that won't be necessary."

"But she's so young," my mother protested. "There's too much at risk for a home birth."

Kara cried out as another contraction washed over her, and Sybil began bustling around the bed, moving blankets and laying out towels. "Sit her up," she demanded of me, and

I pulled at Kara's hands, urging her to rise. Sybil wadded a couple more pillows behind her back.

"There's no time now," Rhea insisted.

"Olivia," my mother said. "We should go."

I looked at her over my shoulder. "No. She needs me. Go get her some water from the kitchen."

Pursing her lips again and casting suspicious glances at Rhea and Sybil, she finally ducked out of the room.

Kara's fingers brushed at my hospital bracelet. "Oh, Olives," she muttered.

I winced, my eyes filling with tears. "I know. Stupid Olivia."

Kara shook her head. "I did that."

I didn't respond.

I'm sorry, she mouthed just before doubling over with the agony of fresh pain.

She panted between contractions, her cries growing louder and more frantic. The time for talking, for reckoning, had passed. Rhea positioned herself between Kara's thighs, rubbing at the tired muscles and coaxing her daughter through an impossible labor.

For my part, I simply held on, feeling Kara's grip tighten enough to crush bone and then go slack again and again.

Sybil collapsed in a chair behind us, rocking and humming some tune from a forgotten past.

My mother ran small errands, fetching things for Rhea, then pacing the back of the room, a reluctant spectator.

Forty minutes later, Kara screamed, her cry the howl of a dying animal, as she leaned against me and the baby emerged in a slick of blood right into Rhea's waiting arms.

"She's here," Rhea shouted, wiping frantically, her hands working at the speed of light, cleaning, cutting, ensuring the first breath followed by the low cries of life.

"A girl," I whispered to Kara, my face lighting with half a smile, the adrenaline of the moment flooding my veins.

"Always," she whispered back.

The dark words she'd spoken of their curse rippled back to me, a shroud over the elation circling us. I still didn't fully understand what she meant, but I was beginning to see my way to a theory. The haunted house, the near-dead bird, the tunnel to nowhere and her incoherent rambling, the death row pen pals, and the morbid drive within her building like the hum of a swarm, the thundering of drums and hooves on a funeral march.

I knew this baby's father; I'd seen him once before, under the water, the day my brother drowned. Kara made it to her destination all right—she met with the man with the camera. And she'd said herself I was right. Anyone else would never have returned from that date. But the Hallases were something older, darker. Where the rest of us see a dead end, they see only a continuum of possibility. Kara's curse—her *truth*—would carry her away in the end, I realized with blinding clarity. But in her time here, it had also saved me.

That's when I felt it steal into the room like a cold mist. I turned from the exhaustion on my friend's face. He was an icy vacuum, more felt than seen, the absence of all warmth. Sybil stood before her chair, both arms outstretched, her face open, expectant, as she took a shaky step forward and then another. For a moment, the milky veils that covered her eyes parted, and a history flickered there like an old film reel, lit from within.

I opened my mouth to warn her *Not another step*, but paths that are destined to collide cannot be thwarted, not for long. What would I have spared her? An hour? A moment?

The hush at the heart of every winter stole her last steps, her last breaths. The light within snuffed out. Just before she fell, the fog of her eyes met mine, and there was nothing in them.

Her drop was a clatter of small bones, barely a thud.

My mother screamed.

Rhea stiffened, her face waxen, and rushed to her too late.

Kara leaned back, taking her child up in her arms, sucking the life and light in every corner of the room into her aura, until she glowed without mercy.

She never even saw the old woman fall.

CHAPTER 32

Newborns have the sweetest breath, like clover and cream. I'd nearly forgotten since Robby died, but Kara's baby seemed to sweep into the world on a cloud of oxytocin and happy memories, despite the bleak circumstances surrounding her birth. She curled against her mother's breast in a sleepy daze of perfect trust.

I twirled my finger insider her tiny palm, feeling the little bones of her own fingers clutching mine. I smiled up at Kara from where I sat huddled next to them on the bed. "She's perfect."

"Right?" Kara petted her cheek. "Everything makes sense when I look at her."

The paramedics had taken Sybil's body away an hour earlier. Rhea had run out to an all-night store for a few necessities, and my mother was downstairs making tea in the Hallases' kitchen.

"When Robby was born, he was so red and wrinkly he

looked like a sun-dried tomato. I'd nearly forgotten about that. And they put this little hat on him at the hospital that made him look like a baby gnome."

Kara beamed, then looked into my eyes with a weight she hadn't shown since I'd last seen her. "He'll always be perfect, Olives. No matter what happens, Robby will always be his perfect, beautiful self. Nothing can take that away."

"I know," I reassured her. And I did. Something inside me had shifted in the last few days, the way a log in the fire finally weakens and falls away with a loud crack, sending a few bright sparks into the air. "And so will she."

Kara grinned, staring into the tiny copy of her own face snuggled in her arms.

"What are you going to name her?"

"Olivia?" she said, raising a brow, and we both laughed until the baby began to squirm.

"No," she said finally, after getting her resettled. "Something happy though. Something lively. She deserves a name like that. She's my do-over."

"Your do-over?"

"You know, the proverbial second wind, the phoenix rising from the ashes. That's how she feels, like a fresh start."

"I'm sorry about Sybil," I whispered, concerned that Kara hadn't fully registered her grandmother's loss.

"Don't be. She had a long life, and she's home now. And in a way, she's still here, in this little bundle in my arms." She nuzzled her baby closer as she spoke.

I nodded. "We'll have to think of something to tell Prescott."

Kara glanced up at me. "Oh?"

"This is…well, it's sudden to say the least. He'll come around eventually, and he'll have questions."

"I think you should tell him."

"Tell him what?"

Kara's eyes found mine, and there was a haze of regret in them. "Tell him the truth. Tell him that two girls, who loved each other, also loved him. Tell him that one moved on, and the other didn't. Tell him that he has your heart, Olives, even if she has mine."

I nodded, suddenly unable to find words, as if my gut was registering something my brain still hadn't picked up on.

"I'm glad you two will have each other."

"Where are you going?" I asked quietly.

Kara looked at me. "Nowhere. But it's not exactly like I'll be breaking into pools with the two of you anymore, is it?" She reached out to squeeze my hand. "I can't thank you enough, Olivia."

"For what?"

"For this, for everything. For being here for me tonight. For letting me in."

I wanted to tell her that I was the one who owed her the thank-you. I wanted to tell her that my heart was still hers, even if everything had changed like she'd warned me it would that night she turned up in my room soaking wet. I wanted to talk about plans for the baby and how I could come over after school in the afternoons and sit in Sybil's old chair and rock and rock with her child in my arms.

But none of it felt right in my mouth. None of it seemed strong enough to live outside the chambers of my own heart.

And so I swallowed everything I wanted to tell her and focused my gaze on the impossible new life balled up in a blanket beside her.

"I know what you should name her," I said, feeling one small thing float up and out of my throat with enough energy to be heard. "Zoe."

Kara looked up from her small bundle to me and flashed a smile. "Zoe," she repeated, trying it out.

"Doesn't it mean life or something like that?"

"Yeah, it's perfect. *Zoe*."

CHAPTER 33

In a way, I think I always knew they would be gone.

I'd long since given up believing the Hallas women operated by the same universal laws as the rest of us. Cursed or gifted, they were woven from a fabric apart, spun into being on a loom lost in time, a relic of Mount Olympus or Shambhala or bubbled up from an overpopulated underworld. Their touch had freed me from purgatory on earth. I could feel little but gratitude to be a stop along the way to whatever cycle destiny held for them next.

I kicked through the empty rooms, my sneaker catching only lint on carpet, the memories of the night before haunting me like a still-fresh dream. Once Kara took up her child, she didn't need my hand anymore. Rhea was making arrangements as I escorted my mother out, her shoulders trembling under my grip. We fell into bed, assuring ourselves all would be well, we'd check in the morning.

Morning came late. And when I had finally eaten and

dressed and convinced my parents that it was safe for me to check in on Kara, just for a short while, I found the house across the street empty of all but its memories.

I knew the second I saw Sybil's rocker was gone, but I pushed my way in through the front door anyhow. Her little smoking room was silent, the kitchen lights out. Even the plant I'd once brought over was missing. The stairwell stretched like a lazy cat into nothing. Rhea's bedroom held only the infamous rafters. I stood now in Kara's room, empty as one of those Easter egg shells that they pierce to blow the yolk out.

Except for one thing.

In the middle of the floor, where I once sat at the end of her bed, her lips on mine, was my grandmother's ring. The white gold band flashed its embrace around the aquamarine. I walked over and picked it up, understanding. This was Kara's goodbye. It wasn't an accident. She didn't leave it behind in a rush. I could feel the warmth of her fingers still on it as I pressed it to my palm. She left this for me, a gesture worth a thousand letters.

I slipped it onto my middle finger, a perfect fit.

The sky cracked outside, filling the empty rooms with echoing thunder. I raced down to the front door just in time to see the first drops fall. I'd thought the gray of the morning was from residual smoke still hanging in the air. I'd missed the clouds amassing overhead, the kiss of humidity on my skin. I watched from the front porch for a while, sitting cross-legged where Sybil's rocker had once been. Even dead, I could still feel her boiled-egg eyes on me and read the smile of her knowing in the patterns of the raindrops.

Across from me, the live oak still stood, as if proclaiming our rebirth.

Six weeks passed. Another year of high school was at my door. My mother had come home only yesterday, clean and tremulous as a new leaf. We embraced her gently, but her hugs back were firm. She was here to stay.

Dr. Brandt assured me the first few days would be exciting, new, even awkward, but that routine would settle soon enough. I would have to adjust to having a mother again. Not because she'd been in rehab for over a month, but because she'd been all but absent for the last three years. It would take a while, he said. I might not like her asserting herself again. But he was wrong. It was good to be seen. When her eyes found mine, I knew I was real to her, to myself.

My mother wasn't the only one to return to us. A few weeks after the fire, a man turned up at our door clutching a blackened, soapstone urn. They'd found it among the rubble and used Robby's name to trace it to us. My father went out the same day and bought a special cabinet for it that we put in a well-lit corner of the living room, where Robby should have been the last three years. I like to think he sent it to us, so we'd never forget, so we'd know he was always close.

Dr. Brandt, for his part, did his best to understand what led to my overdose. He was the counselor I'd been assigned—a patient man, over sixty, with a slight frame and an even slighter lisp. He wore cardigan sweaters no matter how hot it was outside, and he spoke very slowly, as if pondering every word.

His appointments always relaxed me.

Of course, there were things I could never explain to him, things he would never understand. Things I barely understood myself. He understood Kara to be my friend who'd recently moved, an impulsive girl and a bad influence. No more.

For my part, I didn't understand her much better. I would never be able to explain what drove her, the machinations behind her obsessions, her compulsion. I would never make heads or tails of her disappearance and the child that followed. Or why she came at all. Did I draw her here? My family with one foot in Robby's grave? Was I just another inmate, locked behind bars of grief?

Dr. Brandt said the establishment termed it *complicated grief*, but he had his own word for it—*breech* grieving. It's when the process sticks somewhere, like a bone in the throat. We get all turned around in it, backward and perpetual, with no clear way forward. He said situations like ours call for a skilled hand to reach in and turn the soul, so that passage through the grief cycle can be accomplished.

But he made sure I understood that we would never be completely free of the pain of losing my brother. "You will circle back through the emotions many times in your life, Olivia. Grief is like a staircase. You get off on one floor, but you can only travel so far before you have to face the stairs again and take the next flight up."

I liked to think of Kara that way—a maddening elevator ride, pummeling through floor after floor of my loss, a midwife for my soul.

Prescott was waiting in his driveway, drumming his fingers on the roof of his car. "You ready?"

I walked lazily toward him, Samson dancing in circles at my heels. I had finally answered his texts a few days before. "Sure you want to do this? It's not too late to back out, you know."

He smirked. "Just get in the car, Olives."

His mother ran out to collect the dog. "Oh, Olivia! How are you, dear? How's your mom? She's back home now, right?"

I nodded, trying to not laugh at Prescott rolling his eyes in the corner of my vision. "She's fine. Thanks. You should go see her. She'd like that."

"Oh, well, I suppose I could do that, sure." Her expression was more uncertain than her words.

"Mom, take Samson inside. We have to go or we'll be late."

I opened the passenger door, enjoying the shine of the aquamarine on my finger as it caught the morning sunlight.

"Okay, okay," she dismissed him. "You two have a great first day back at school."

Prescott rolled his eyes again and ducked into the car.

I buckled the seat belt over me as he backed out of the drive, the Hallases' house filling the rearview mirror as an agent hammered a new For Sale sign into the front lawn.

Prescott lowered his brows as he watched for a moment. "Guess that's it then. She won't be back."

"No. She won't." We hadn't talked much about what happened that night when I walked in on them, just enough to make clear that there was understanding and forgiveness on both sides. "Disappointed?"

He shrugged. "Do you ever feel like she wasn't real at all?

Like maybe you just imagined the whole thing? But then you think how fucked up your mind would be to make all that up?"

I laughed. "She was real. Say whatever else you want about her, but she was real."

Prescott shifted his eyes from their house to the ring on my hand. "Do you miss her?"

I scrunched up my nose a little as I let the truth slip out with my breath. "Every day."

"I never got to tell her goodbye. Did you?"

I twisted the aquamarine around my finger, recalling the sweetness of her breath in our last moments, the fullness of her presence. "I think so."

"I missed you too, Olivia."

I smiled into Prescott's face. "I know."

"But I don't really miss the Resurrection Girls."

I took a breath as he drove away. Neither did I.

ACKNOWLEDGMENTS

My lovely family. Evelyn, where would this story be without you? I shudder to think. You are in every page. Your tireless cheerleading, creative ideas, and sparkling laughter are something I will miss each and every time I sit down to my laptop. I wish you were here for this part. You deserve to be. Zoey and Ben, I could not have gone on without you each holding me up, helping me find my smile and my voice after the world exploded around us. Thank you for being my reason to keep breathing and keep writing. Nathan, there isn't a word for the level of loyalty and support you have shown. There isn't a word for how I love you. Thank you for giving me something to hang onto in the dark.

My brilliant agent, Thao Le, who has stood by me through enough twists, dips, and falls to fill a theme park. I hit the agent jackpot when I found you. I am forever grateful for your thoughtful guidance. You have made me a deeper thinker and a better writer. And most importantly, I will never forget your kindness and patience when I shifted from just writing about child loss to living it. It means the world to me that you believe in my work.

My editors, Eliza Swift, Christina Pulles, and the team at Albert Whitman. Thank you, Eliza, for being the first one to fall in love with Kara and Olivia and taking a chance on their story. I'm so grateful for the opportunity you have given my characters and my writing. Thank you, Christina, for jumping in with both feet and making this project your own. I am incredibly proud of how you and your team have made this story shine.

And finally, the bereaved community who has surrounded me with more love and compassion than I ever knew existed. *We do not walk alone.* To every family who has felt the crush of child loss—I see you. I see your shattered hearts and hold them next to mine. I know your pain as my own. I draw every ragged breath beside you. I did not start this book as one of you, but I finished it that way. Thank you for sharing your journeys and stories and children with me and listening as I shared mine with you.

AVA MORGYN is a native Texan who grew up falling in love with all the wrong characters in all the wrong stories. She is a lover of crystals, tarot, and powerful women with bad reputations. She studied English writing and rhetoric at St. Edward's University in Austin and currently resides with her family in Houston, where she lives surrounded by books and rocks and writes a blog on child loss, forloveofevelyn.com. You can visit her website at www.avamorgyn.com.